If only I could ride him myself...

"Come on, Aladdin," Ashleigh shouted. "Show them what you've got!" She watched every move the big colt made, feeling as though she were right there with him. In her mind she could see herself riding Aladdin, stretching him to his limit, the two of them working as a single unit, traveling faster than the wind.

Peter and Aladdin approached the quarter-mile pole by the bleachers. Ashleigh could hear the colt's steam-engine-like huffs as he flew past them, heading for the final turn into the stretch. Ashleigh held her breath in anticipation.

But Aladdin's stride began to go more up and down than forward, his hind legs dragging and his knees flailing. Ashleigh recognized the mooselike way of going that Mike had mentioned. Peter flapped his arm behind him, trying to urge the horse on, but there was no noticeable change. The colt had slowed visibly. Peter gave up and hand-rode to the finish line, scrubbing the reins up and down Aladdin's neck in an effort to drive the colt on.

Mike clicked the stopwatch. "His time's not very impressive. He's going to have to do better than this to get a piece of that race on Saturday.

Collect all the books in the Thoroughbred series

Collect all the books in the Ashleigh series

* coming soon

THOROUGHBRED

Ashleigh

THE FORBIDDEN STALLION

CREATED BY

JOANNA CAMPBELL

WRITTEN BY

CHRIS PLATT

HarperEntertainment
A Division of HarperCollins*Publishers*

HarperEntertainment
A Division of HarperCollins*Publishers*
10 East 53rd Street, New York, NY 10022-5299

This is a work of fiction. The characters, incidents, and dialogues are products of the author's imagination and are not to be construed as real. Any resemblance to actual events or persons, living or dead, is entirely coincidental.

In loving memory of
James Kelley, Tom Cleveland, and Raymond Horn

Produced by 17th Street Productions,
a division of Daniel Weiss Associates, Inc.

ISBN 0-06-10-6558-7

HarperCollins®, 📖®, and HarperEntertainment™ are trademarks of HarperCollins Publishers Inc.

Cover art © 1999 by Daniel Weiss Associates, Inc.

First printing: August 1999

Printed in the United States of America

Visit HarperEntertainment on the World Wide Web at
http://www.harpercollins.com

❖ 10 9 8 7 6 5 4 3

1

"Hurry up, Ashleigh!" Mona Gardener called from outside Edgardale's large brown barn. "It looks like it's going to rain soon. We'd better hurry."

Ashleigh Griffen poked her head out the stable door and smiled at her best friend. Mona was riding Frisky, her beautiful bay Thoroughbred mare. Ashleigh and Mona were both horse-crazy. A little Kentucky rain would never stop them from riding. But Ashleigh's parents didn't see it that way. If it started to rain before the girls left, they wouldn't be allowed to go.

By the look of the low-hanging clouds, they might get in an hour of riding before the rains started.

A gust of March wind blew Ashleigh's long, dark hair across her face. "I'll be out in a minute, Mona," she called to her friend. "I have to help my mom and dad bring the broodmares in. You can ride Frisky in the front paddock while you're waiting," she suggested.

A gruff voice echoed down the barn aisle. "March came in like a lamb, but it's going to go out like a lion," Edgardale's hired hand, Jonas, observed as he pulled a lead rope from its hook on the wall. "You two get going, Ashleigh. I'll help your folks with the broodmares." Ashleigh smiled at the old stable hand. Jonas had come to work at the Griffens' Thoroughbred breeding farm several months earlier, when their other hired man, Kurt, left to work on his sister's farm.

"Thanks, Jonas, but I have to do my share of the chores," Ashleigh said. "That was part of the bargain I made when my parents agreed to let me keep Stardust." She grabbed another lead rope from the wall and stroked the pretty chestnut mare that stood in crossties as she passed.

Mrs. Griffen stepped out of the tack room with an armful of halters. "Don't forget that schoolwork was also a part of that deal," she reminded Ashleigh. "Make sure you're home in plenty of time to do your math before dinner." She handed two of the halters to Ashleigh and several to Jonas.

Ashleigh nodded. Her math grade had dropped so much lately that her parents had told her she either had to get the grade up to an acceptable level immediately or be grounded, unable to ride Stardust, until her grade went up.

Ashleigh cringed at the thought. She wanted to be a jockey someday—how could she accomplish that if she couldn't ride? She shook off the horrible thought and headed for Go Gen's paddock.

The gray mare lifted her elegant head and nickered a greeting as Ashleigh approached. She patted the mare and smiled. Go Gen was due to foal any day now, and she was big as a house. Her foal would be the first one of the season, and everyone at the Edgardale breeding farm was excited—even her older sister, Caroline, who wasn't as interested in the horses as the rest of the family.

This year the Griffens were starting a new tradition: Everyone would make a guess at what each newborn foal's color would be. The winner got to name the foal, and had control of the television set for an hour after dinner every night for a week.

Ashleigh grinned as she stood on tiptoe to buckle Go Gen's halter. She knew which show she would pick if she won: *Old Red And Me,* the only show on TV starring a boy and his horse. Even Caroline liked the show, but only because she thought the boy who starred in it was cute.

Ashleigh had bet that Go Gen's colt would be gray, like its dam. Caroline guessed the foal would be a dark bay, but Rory wanted it to be black, because that had been the color of his favorite colt, Midnight Wanderer.

A cloud of sadness passed over Ashleigh at the thought of the yearling colt they'd had to put down the month before because of his broken back leg. The memory still hurt, but she knew they had made the right decision. The leg hadn't been healing, and the colt had been in a lot of pain.

Ashleigh put Go Gen in her stall and went back for Rory's pony, Moe. The Shetland turned his molasses-colored rump on her and took off to the other end of the paddock, cropping grass as quickly as he could. Moe was up to his tricks again.

"Leave him alone until all the mares are in," Mr. Griffen called from the side of the barn, where he and Ashleigh's older sister, Caroline, were unloading bags of grain from the farm's old truck. He wiped his hand across his brow, pushing the dark hair off his forehead as he laughed at the pony's antics. Ashleigh was the only child in the family with her father's dark coloring. Rory and Caroline were both blond, like their mother.

Derek Griffen grabbed the heavy feed bag that Caroline had pulled to the edge of the truck's tailgate. He hefted the bag over his shoulder and smiled at Ashleigh. "Don't worry about Moe," he assured her.

"When he sees that everyone else is in the barn, he'll come running."

"Yeah," five-year-old Rory mimicked his father as he held open the feed shed door. "He'll come running."

As predicted, Moe waited until the last mare was in the barn before trotting up to the gate, Kentucky bluegrass hanging out the sides of his mouth.

"You're silly," Ashleigh said as she opened the gate to lead the pony into his stall. "Can I ride Stardust now?" she called down the aisle to her mother.

Elaine Griffen looked up from the stall she was mucking out and nodded. "Sure, Ashleigh. Just make sure you're not gone too long. I'd like to see you finish your homework before dinner. Your father and I are expecting a good grade on that math test tomorrow. I'm sure Stardust is, too," her mother added, reminding Ashleigh of their agreement.

Ashleigh could do that problem—a bad grade equaled no riding. "Don't worry, Mom," she called as she hurried to where Stardust was standing in crossties. Hastily she picked out the mare's feet, slid the saddle on her back, tightened the girth halfway, and pulled her bridle off its peg. Stardust lowered her head and accepted the bit.

"Good girl," Ashleigh whispered as she pulled the headstall over the mare's ears, thinking of how difficult Stardust had been when she'd first arrived.

Several months earlier, Stardust wouldn't even walk with her, and the mare had thrown Ashleigh many times. But thanks to some great training videos and the help of her mother, father, and Jonas, Stardust was turning out to be a nice mount and a great friend.

Jonas held Stardust's head with one hand and swung Ashleigh into the saddle with the other.

"Thanks, Jonas," Ashleigh said as she buckled on her riding helmet and poked her toes into the stirrups. Mona saw her and trotted Frisky over from the paddock.

"Have a nice ride," Mrs. Griffen called, waving to the girls as they trotted out of the stable yard and down the fence-lined gravel drive. "Your father and I have a nice surprise to tell everyone at dinner tonight. Don't be late."

A surprise? Ashleigh looked at Mona and grinned. Ashleigh's parents liked giving surprises almost as much as she and Rory and Caroline liked getting them. *I wonder what it is.*

She turned in the saddle to shout the question back to her mother, but a big gust of wind blew sharply, kicking up dead leaves and making Stardust jump. Ashleigh grabbed a handful of mane and turned her attention back to her mount. Stardust arched her neck and cocked her tail, prancing smartly.

Mona laughed. "She's such a clown! You'd better hold on tight, Ash. It looks like we're in for a fun ride today!"

Ashleigh laughed, too, and shortened her reins to bring the mare back under control. When a cold breeze was blowing, the horses always felt good. She took a deep breath of the cool rain-scented air and smiled. Stardust wasn't the only one who felt good that day. Ashleigh always felt great when she could ride her very own horse!

Ashleigh looked with pride across the rolling white-fenced pastures of Edgardale, her home. It wouldn't be long before spring sunshine turned the pastures to lush, deep stretches of Kentucky bluegrass and that year's crop of new foals were romping with their dams across the paddocks.

"Where do you want to go today?" Mona asked, interrupting Ashleigh's thoughts.

"How about if we ride in the fields behind your house?" Ashleigh suggested. "We haven't been back there since that logging company removed all those old trees. We could go and see what they did."

"Great idea," Mona said. She turned Frisky onto an old dirt road and nudged her into a canter. Ashleigh followed close behind.

They pulled the mares to a halt at the top of the rise. "Wow!" Ashleigh exclaimed as she looked out over the logging site. She moved Stardust forward, surveying all the stumps. The scent of freshly cut pine filled her nose and she breathed deeply. "It smells just like Christmas."

"It really does," Mona agreed. "Look." She pointed to the end of the clearing. "They left a few logs. They look like they'd make good jumps, don't they?"

Ashleigh walked Stardust over to the felled logs. They were only about two feet off the ground. The jumps Mona's mother had set up in their ring were much higher.

"Let's jump them," Mona suggested.

"What?" Ashleigh swung Stardust around to face her friend. "That's easy for you to say—you've had lessons. I don't know how to jump."

"Oh, come on, Ash," Mona prodded. "Horses jump stuff in the pastures all the time. You just need to lean forward a little and stay off her mouth while she's going over the jump."

"I don't know." Ashleigh shook her head and backed Stardust away from the log. "I don't feel very good about this."

"I'm going to try it," Mona said as she moved Frisky forward, letting the mare sniff the log before turning her around and backtracking up the field.

"Be careful," Ashleigh warned.

Mona trotted Frisky toward the log. When they

reached the jump, the bay mare hesitated for only a split second before picking up her white-stockinged feet and springing nimbly over the downed pine tree.

"Yes!" Ashleigh shouted in unison with her friend as Mona circled the mare and approached the log again. This time Frisky didn't even flinch before sailing over the jump. The pair looked like they were flying!

Mona reined Frisky in next to Stardust. "It's a blast, Ash. You've got to try it!" she cried.

All lingering doubt disappeared as Ashleigh caught Mona's excitement. "It does look like a lot of fun," she said as she patted Stardust's neck and rode toward the starting point. "Let's do it, girl."

"Give Stardust her head a few strides before you reach the jump," Mona instructed.

Ashleigh asked her mare for a trot, posting in time to the stride. Stardust pricked her ears and warily approached the jump. Three strides before the log Ashleigh loosened the reins and leaned forward, as Mona had done. At that moment Stardust snorted and slammed on the brakes.

Fortunately, Ashleigh was properly balanced and had her heels down. She flopped in the saddle a few times, but she stayed on.

"I don't think she wants to do this," Ashleigh said. "Maybe I shouldn't make her."

"It's not a good idea to let her get away with a refusal," Mona said as she brought her mare up to stand next to Stardust. "Maybe she just needs a little more help from you to get her over it."

"How do I do that?" Ashleigh asked.

"My teacher told me that when a horse refuses, you should use a lot of leg and trot all the way up to the jump," Mona explained. "Don't loosen your reins until just before she picks her feet up to go over the jump. If she doesn't have her head, it will give her less of a chance to refuse. Once she learns to trust your judgment, then you can let her have her head sooner."

"But what if she stops again?" Ashleigh asked.

Mona shrugged. "She can do it, Ash. Let her try again."

Ashleigh took a deep breath and patted Stardust's neck. "Come on, girl. You trust me, don't you?"

She circled Stardust, aiming her toward the jump. This time Ashleigh kept her legs on the girth, forcing the mare to move forward, and guiding her with the reins. At the spot where Stardust had balked before, Ashleigh applied a little more leg pressure. Stardust popped straight up and landed hard on the other side. It wasn't perfect form, but they'd done it—they'd cleared the jump!

"Way to go, Ash!" Mona cheered.

"That was great! I want to do it again," Ashleigh

said as she ruffled Stardust's mane. "See, you can trust me, girl," she called to the chestnut. Stardust shook her head and snorted, her ears pricked with excitement.

They spent the next twenty minutes taking turns jumping the logs. When the first raindrops began to fall, they called it quits.

"Time to go," Ashleigh called, pointing Stardust toward Edgardale.

The girls parted when they reached Mona's driveway. Stardust tossed her head in protest at the loss of her friend, but she listened to Ashleigh's commands and trotted toward home.

"Don't forget to study for the big math test tomorrow," Mona called after her through the drizzling rain.

Ashleigh waved to her friend over her shoulder. How could she forget? So much depended on this test. If she didn't pass it, her parents would ground her. And after all the fun they'd just had, the thought of not being able to ride was unimaginable.

The warmth of the hallway entrance felt wonderful on Ashleigh's chilled face and fingers. She took off her wet coat and rubbed her hands together.

Her ride had lasted longer than she had planned,

and from the sound of dishes clanking in the kitchen and pungent odor of garlic, dinner was nearly ready. Ashleigh felt a twinge of guilt. She should have gotten at least a half hour's worth of studying done before dinner. Now it was too late; she'd have to wait until after dinner.

"Mmm. What smells so good?" Ashleigh asked as she pulled off her riding boots.

"Spaghetti," Mrs. Griffen answered. "Your father and I had to pull a bunch of hay down from the loft. We were running a little late, so Caroline made dinner tonight. It looks delicious."

Caroline beamed at the compliment.

"Wash your hands and get out of those wet clothes," Mrs. Griffen said. "Your father has something to tell everyone, and he wants to wait until we're all sitting down."

Ashleigh nodded and then turned to take the stairs two at a time. What would the surprise be? Maybe their father had gotten tickets to this year's Kentucky Derby. Even Caroline loved to attend that race. She didn't care much about riding, but she loved to get dressed up and look important.

She returned to the table and took her seat just as the first helping of spaghetti was served. "Thanks, Mom." Ashleigh took the plate her mother handed to her. She picked up her fork and took a quick bite of the pasta-and-tomato concoction. "It *is* good, Caro," she said to her sister.

Spaghetti was one of Ashleigh's favorite meals, but with her stomach doing flip-flops in anticipation of her parents' surprise, she didn't know how much more she could eat.

Caroline was the first to speak.

"Well?"

"Well, what?" Mr. Griffen stabbed a meatball and popped it into his mouth.

"The surprise!" Rory beat everyone to the punch. "What's the surprise?"

Mr. Griffen wiped some spaghetti sauce off his chin. "All right, everybody, listen up," he said as he tapped his knife against the side of his glass. He turned to Ashleigh. "This announcement should be especially interesting to you, Ashleigh." Mr. Griffen cleared his throat. "As everyone knows, two years ago we sold Aladdin's Treasure to the Danworths in Florida."

Ashleigh's breath caught in her throat. Aladdin! She had been so preoccupied the past few months with her new horse, and Midnight's death, that she had forgotten to check the *Daily Racing Form* to see if the three-year-old colt had started racing.

Ashleigh's heart felt as though it were galloping in her chest. "Wha-What about Aladdin?" she managed to sputter out.

Mr. Griffen smiled. "Aladdin is running in a stakes race at Hialeah this Saturday. The Danworths are sending their private jet for us early that morning. We're going to watch Aladdin race."

Ashleigh could hardly contain herself. Aladdin was her dream horse. She had done hours of research with her mother and father to determine which stallion would be the best match for Aladdin's dam, Go Gen. She had picked the same sire as Wanderer's Quest, one of their best fillies, who had gone on to win the Florida Derby at Gulfstream Park a month earlier.

She knew the beautiful black colt with four white socks and a blaze would be a champion someday—just like Quest. Oh, how she had begged her father to keep Aladdin so that Edgardale could start racing their own horses. She knew that the big black colt was destined to be a champion, and now she was actually going to get to see him race!

"We're going to ride in a plane!" Rory hollered as he raced around the table with his arms outstretched like the wings of plane.

"A private jet!" Caroline said with awe. "I knew the Danworths were rich, but I didn't know they were *that* rich. I'll have to pack my best clothes. How long will we be there?"

Mrs. Griffen snagged Rory on his next flight around the table and guided him back to his chair.

"We're going to the race, and then the Danworths have invited us to have dinner with them before we fly back. We'll pack tomorrow night, but not too much stuff, Caro—we'll only be gone for the day."

Ashleigh stuffed a forkful of spaghetti into her mouth. It was hard to eat and smile at the same time, but she couldn't keep the smile off her face. What a great surprise!

"What do you think, Ashleigh?" Derek Griffen asked his younger daughter. "I know you pinned a lot of hopes on this colt."

Ashleigh swung her legs back and forth under her chair. She felt like a racehorse ready to charge out of the gate. "I'll miss Stardust, but I can't wait to see Aladdin," she gushed. "And we're going to watch him win a stakes race!"

"Well . . . ," Mrs. Griffen said, and paused. "I wouldn't get my expectations up that high."

Ashleigh's fork paused midway to her mouth. "What do you mean?" she demanded. "Aladdin's been winning all his races, hasn't he? He's one of the best colts we've raised." She watched her parents exchange glances.

Mr. Griffen took a drink of water and set his glass down, seeming to consider his words carefully. "Aladdin has been . . . how do I put this?" He looked Ashleigh straight in the eye. "Aladdin has been somewhat of a disappointment to the Danworths. It appears that he doesn't have the run in him that we thought he might. The best he's run is the middle of the pack."

Ashleigh's fork clattered to her plate and her heart dropped to her shoes. "How can that be? He's bred to be a champion, just like Quest. What are they doing wrong?"

"Why would they fly us all the way down to Florida to watch a losing horse?" Caroline asked.

Mrs. Griffen shook her head. "They're not sure if it's the horse or the training. They've got a new trainer, and they're hoping he'll make the difference. If not, Aladdin might be coming home to Edgardale to stand at stud."

A stallion at Edgardale! The silence in the room was so big, it felt as if the moment had been frozen. Ashleigh let out the breath she had been holding, then everyone talked at once. If they brought a stallion to Edgardale, it would mean a major change in the farm's operation, and an opportunity for the farm to expand. Other farms would bring their mares to Edgardale to be bred, and the Griffens could collect big stud fees. It would only be a matter of time before they were training their own racers and Ashleigh was riding them—her dream!

"Okay, okay." Mr. Griffen held his hands up to ward off all the questions. "I know this is quite a surprise.

Mr. Danworth and I have been speaking about this for a while. The deal is, if Aladdin doesn't do well in this race, they are going to give up on his racing career and send him back to stand at stud here at Edgardale. They're hoping that maybe he'll pass on his good genes and his offspring will have the run he was meant to have."

When dinner was over, Ashleigh excused herself, taking her dishes to the kitchen sink.

"Your math book is in the living room," Mrs. Griffen called after her.

Ashleigh searched the living room, spotting the text on the coffee table next to a pile of *Daily Racing Forms*. She paused as she picked up the math book. It wouldn't hurt to look through a couple of the old racing forms before she got started on her math. They followed Thoroughbred racing all over the country, and listed the results of races run in weeks past. If she could find the results of Aladdin's past races, they might provide a clue as to why he was running so poorly.

Ashleigh grabbed the racing forms and ran up the stairs. Math would just have to wait. There was something more important at stake right now—Aladdin's future!

2

Ashleigh looked at the clock on the wall above the teacher's head. The clock was silent, but in her mind the *tick-tick-tick* of the second hand sounded as loud as a horse galloping across the pavement at midnight.

Only five more minutes left on the math test, and she still had at least ten questions to answer. That gave her thirty seconds to answer each question. If only the test were as easy as that.

Ashleigh was furious with herself. She'd spent the entire evening reading old racing forms instead of studying her math. The only time she had even opened her math text was when Caroline had come to bed. Ashleigh had waited until she heard the even sounds of her sister's deep-sleep breathing before pulling out her flashlight and reading the rest of the racing forms under the covers.

Ashleigh heard the scrape of Mona's chair behind

her. She felt her best friend glance over her paper as Mona got up to turn in her test.

"Come on, Ash, you can do it," Mona whispered encouragingly as she passed Ashleigh's desk.

Ashleigh gave her a weak smile and then turned her attention back to the paper in front of her. She tried to concentrate on the problems, but her thoughts soon drifted back to Aladdin. She hadn't found anything about him in the racing forms except poor odds and mediocre finishes in unchallenging races. But Aladdin was from great racing stock—what could be wrong?

"Okay, class." The teacher's voice cut through Ashleigh's thoughts. "Please put your pencils down and pass your papers forward."

Ashleigh gulped as she handed in her paper. There were still ten unanswered questions. She knew what that meant: She was doomed. There would be no more riding Stardust until she could improve her math grade. How long would that take? She sighed heavily. At the rate she was going, it could be eons.

Mona gave her a sympathetic smile. "Well, at least we won't get our tests back until tomorrow. That gives you one last day to ride Stardust before you have to give your parents the bad news."

"Yeah, but after tomorrow it's going to be awful," Ashleigh said as she grabbed her books and shoved them into her bag. "How am I going to last even a week without riding? I can't do it!"

Mona led the way out of the classroom and outside to the school bus. "It's not going to be real great for me either, Ash. You know how much I like riding with you. It just won't be the same without you and Stardust for company."

Ashleigh plopped down on the hard bus seat, tossing her book bag under the seat in front of her, her eyes downcast. "Oh, Mona, I should have let you tutor me."

Mona made a face at the boy behind her, who was kicking the back of their seat. "But you've had all that work to do at the barn, and now you've got Stardust to take care of. You're busier than ever. How could you think about math when you've got all that other stuff to do?" Mona defended her friend.

Ashleigh shrugged. "It's not like I don't try. I mean, I look at my math book a lot, but my mind keeps going back to horses."

"Well, there's still hope." Mona gave her an encouraging smile. "You're not grounded yet. Maybe if you promise to work extra hard and get a tutor, your parents will let you slide this time."

The driver closed the doors as the last student got on the bus, and they lurched ahead, out of the parking lot. Ashleigh stared out the window at the lines of bare-branched trees. She felt as empty as those trees looked.

"Not my parents," Ashleigh said. "They always keep their promises. If I don't improve my math grade, I'll never get to ride. And if I don't ride, I'll never get to be a jockey." The thought lay heavy on her heart. She closed her eyes and leaned her head against the cool glass, fighting back the tears. She didn't feel like talking anymore. She just wanted to get home and ride Stardust.

"Here's your stop," Mona said. "I'll tack Frisky up and be right over. We'd better wear our parkas—it's getting really cold out."

Ashleigh grabbed her bag and stepped off the bus, breaking into a jog as soon as her feet hit the ground. This would be the last chance she had to ride Stardust before she was grounded. Every spare moment counted. She ran up the walk to the white two-story farmhouse and threw open the door.

Caroline looked up in surprise from her place at the kitchen table, her soda poised in midair. "Whoa, Ash. Are the neighbor's dogs chasing you?"

Ashleigh dropped her book bag in the corner and took off her coat. "No, I'm just in a hurry to ride Stardust today. Mona and Frisky will be over soon," she said as she slipped off her school shoes and pulled on her riding boots.

Caroline looked at her sister knowingly. "So, how did the math test go, Ash?" she asked, holding up a plate of cookies.

Ashleigh shook her head at the cookies and looked at the floor.

"Not so good, huh?" Caroline said in a sympathetic tone.

"Yeah, not so good," Ashleigh replied.

"I'm sorry, Ash. I know how much riding Stardust means to you." Caroline tried for a lighter tone. "Even if she does enjoy seeing you lying in the dirt now and then."

Ashleigh attempted a smile, but it didn't feel right on her face.

"Maybe I can help you," Caroline offered. "I guess I should have offered sooner, but I was caught up in my own schoolwork and didn't realize you were in trouble."

Ashleigh zipped up her coat. "Thanks for the offer, Caro. I think I've pretty much blown it for this quarter, but spring break is only a week away, and I'll get a new start after that. I could really use the help."

"Sure, Ash, I'd be happy to. Have a good ride today," Caroline called, and went back to the magazine she had been reading.

Ashleigh smiled as she hunted for her gloves. There were moments when she got so mad at Caro she wanted to shake her, but at times like this, she was glad to have her sister around.

Rory pushed through the door carrying Ashleigh's Maine coon kitten. "Prince Charming sneaked out of the house again," he said.

Ashleigh took the gray and white ball of fur from her younger brother and stroked the kitten under the chin until it purred. "You should stick to the house until you're bigger. Those horses could step on you," she admonished, then set the cat free to roam the house.

"Dad says he wants you to help him with the broodmares, Ashleigh," Rory said as he climbed onto the chair next to Caroline and grabbed a cookie from the plate.

"Could you do me a big favor and put my book bag in my room?" Ashleigh asked.

"Sure, Ash." Rory hopped down from the chair and grabbed Ashleigh's bag. "Since I'm being such a big help, will you help me saddle Moe so I can ride now? Mom says I can't ride unless you or Caro is there, and you know Caro doesn't like horse smell to get on her clothes."

It was on the tip of Ashleigh's tongue to say no. She needed every spare minute she could get to ride Stardust, but she noted the hope in his blue eyes. He would be crushed if she refused him.

"Please, Ash?"

"Okay, you've got a deal." It was hard to say no to another horse lover chasing his dreams. "But it'll have to be a quick ride. Mona's coming over in a little bit and I don't want to make her wait too long."

"Can I go with you?" Rory asked.

"Not today, Rory. Mona and I are going to be going really fast, and Moe can't keep up with the bigger horses."

Ashleigh frowned as she remembered this past Christmas, when Mona had gotten Frisky. It was before Stardust, when Ashleigh was still riding Moe. In a jealous fit, Ashleigh had pushed Moe to his max, trying to prove that she could keep up with the long-legged Thoroughbred. Moe had been hurt, and she had felt terrible. Rory almost hadn't forgiven her for that one.

"You can ride in one of the paddocks today," Ashleigh said. "Maybe when the weather's a little better, we'll go for a trail ride together." She closed the door and raced down to the barn.

"Hi, Dad. Where's Mom?" Ashleigh asked as she grabbed several of the hay nets her father was juggling and carried them into the nearest stalls.

"I'm in here," Mrs. Griffen called from a stall down the way. "We're going to put Go Gen in the foaling stall tonight. She could foal anytime now."

"I hope she waits until we get back from Florida," Ashleigh said.

"I do, too," Jonas's voice cut in as he maneuvered down the aisle, his arms loaded with grain buckets. "I've foaled a lot of these mares by myself, but it's sure a lot nicer to have somebody else around in case there's a problem."

Ashleigh heard the patter of Rory's feet coming down the aisle. She turned to see him plunk his helmet over his red-gold hair. He was smiling and ready to ride.

"Rory wants to ride Moe today," Ashleigh said to her parents. "Mona is bringing Frisky over in a while. Is it okay if I help Rory and then go for a ride with Mona after I'm done helping with the broodmares?" Ashleigh asked, leaving out any mention of her math test. She wouldn't deliver the sad news until they asked. She just had to ride that day.

Mrs. Griffen handed Ashleigh her riding helmet. "I'll take care of the mares if you take care of your little brother. It's nice of you to help him with Moe. He seems to be following in your footsteps as far as the riding goes," she said, and smiled. "There are a couple of stalls that need to be done before the horses are brought in for the night, but you can do that when you get back from your ride."

"Thanks, Mom," Ashleigh said as she gathered Moe's tack and grabbed the bucket of brushes.

Rory brought the pony out and hooked him into the crossties. Then he began the pre-ride ritual of brushing him and picking out his feet. Ashleigh grabbed another brush, hoping to hurry her brother along. Every minute she spent on Moe was a minute lost on Stardust.

Seeing Rory's eager face made Ashleigh feel instantly guilty. He deserved to ride as much as she did. Ashleigh sighed. Her little brother didn't know it yet, but he'd soon have her undivided attention when it came to riding. Once she was grounded and couldn't ride her own horse, she'd have plenty of time to spend with Rory and Moe.

Ashleigh tightened Moe's girth and fastened his little bridle. "Let's go, Rory. Your limousine awaits," she said with a flourish as Rory giggled and stepped into the stirrup.

They headed for the large paddock behind the barn. Ashleigh made Rory walk the pony for several minutes while she gave him pointers on how to hold his hands and how to sit properly in the saddle. Rory was a good little rider, but he still needed reminders on occasion.

When he and Moe were working well together, she asked Rory to trot. "Keep your heels down, and sit straight in the saddle," she said, smiling as her brother immediately corrected himself.

"Can we canter now?" Rory asked. "I like to go fast."

"Sure," Ashleigh answered. "Just don't go too fast. It's a little muddy out here. You don't want Moe to fall down."

When Rory was finished, they walked Moe back to the barn. Ashleigh helped unsaddle the pony before hurrying to tack up Stardust. "Don't forget to brush where the girth went," she called. "We don't want him getting girth itch."

Ashleigh heard Mona trotting up the driveway just as she pulled the girth tight on Stardust's saddle. She unsnapped the chestnut mare from the crossties and led her out of the barn.

"Wow, Frisky is really living up to her name," Ashleigh said as she watched the light bay mare prance across the lawn, her four white stockings lifting high into the air. "Better hang on tight."

Ashleigh led Stardust over to the stump at the edge of the driveway and mounted up. A large lump settled in her throat. This would be the last time she would get to ride Stardust for a long while. They had better make it a good one.

Stardust caught the other horse's excitement and started a dance of her own. Ashleigh laughed in spite of herself. It was hard to stay sad when she was riding.

She reined the mare toward the trails at the edge of

the Griffens' property. "Let's head toward the back fields. There's that dirt road we can gallop on. I think they need a good run today."

They started off at a trot, making sure their horses would be warmed up before they let them run. At the last turn in the trail, Mona pulled up beside her and waited for the signal to turn the horses loose.

"Let's go!" Ashleigh called, bending low over her mare's neck and asking for speed. The trees lining the road flashed past as the cool breeze whipped her face. Tears from the wind streamed down her face as Stardust's mane tickled her nose and chin. She was really going to miss this in the weeks to come.

Mona's long-legged Thoroughbred galloped up alongside her, and she smiled over at Ashleigh. Both girls knew that Frisky could outrun Stardust, but Mona held her steady and they crossed the finish line—an old oak tree at the end of the stretch—together.

"That was great!" Ashleigh exclaimed. "I can't wait until I'm riding in a real race!"

They slowed the horses to a walk, letting them cool off. The evening temperature was dropping and the horses' breaths came out in large plumes of frost, like dragons.

"See that field over there?" Ashleigh pointed to the large, flat field that ran behind her house.

Mona nodded her head as she blew into her hands to warm them.

"That's where I want to put Edgardale's training track." Ashleigh waited for that to sink in. When she saw her friend's eyes widen, she continued. "It's not a for-sure thing yet. I keep bugging my dad—I think we could do the broodmares *and* train and race our own horses."

"That would be perfect!" Mona said, her voice filled with the same excitement as Ashleigh's. "And if Aladdin comes to Edgardale, you could be racing his babies." Ashleigh had told Mona all about the beautiful black stallion. And as much as she liked the idea of him standing at stud there at Edgardale, she just couldn't get over the fact that Aladdin hadn't been running well. Something was wrong.

"I don't know," Ashleigh said, changing her tone as she reached out to stroke Stardust's coppery neck. "My dad says it's better to just do one thing well, and we do produce great foals."

"He's got a point," Mona said. "But it would still be great to have your own training track." She pointed to the sinking sun on the horizon. "We'd better head back, Ash," she said. "I know you want to stay out on Stardust for as long as you can, but my mom wasn't very happy about my riding in the rain yesterday. I don't want to get into trouble again."

"Yeah," Ashleigh agreed as she turned her mare back in the direction they had come from and asked for a trot. "It's starting to get dark. If I don't get home before the sun sets, I won't have to wait for my parents to see my math test before I get grounded from riding."

"You can say that again," Mona agreed. She nudged Frisky into a trot and bent into the wind.

Fifteen minutes later they rode into Edgardale, with just enough light left for Mona to make it home. Ashleigh turned Stardust in the direction of the barn. "I'll see you on the bus tomorrow," she called, and halted the mare in front of the barn. The lump was back in her throat again. Who knew how long it would be before she got to ride Stardust again? She leaned forward, laying her cheek against the mare's mane, and wrapped her arms around the chestnut's neck. She never wanted to dismount.

"I'm so sorry, Stardust," Ashleigh cried. "I should have studied harder, but I wanted to spend more time with you." She sat up and ruffled the mare's soft reddish mane. "I could have done a lot of homework last night, but . . ." Ashleigh wiped the back of her hand across her eyes and stifled a sob. "The worst part is that it was all for nothing. There wasn't anything I read that will help Aladdin. If I'd been studying math all that time, I might have finished those last ten problems."

Ashleigh hugged the mare one more time and then dismounted, leading Stardust into the barn. It was empty except for the horses. *Good,* she thought. She didn't feel like company at the moment.

She untacked Stardust and brushed her until her coat shone. When it was time to put the mare back in her stall, Ashleigh promised to spend as much time with her as she could even if she couldn't ride. Maybe her parents would even let her do her math homework at the desk in the tack room.

Several of the broodmares nickered as Ashleigh got out a can of grain for Stardust. Ashleigh noticed that they were all in their stalls, and every stall had already been mucked out. She frowned and wiped a tear from her cheek. She had been out riding for so long that someone else had cleaned her stalls. It looked like she was in trouble again.

3

ASHLEIGH LOLLED IN BED WHEN THE ALARM SOUNDED THE next morning. She usually rose quickly and raced to help Jonas feed the horses before breakfast, but this was the day she would get her math test back. She didn't see any rush to start the day, not when it would end with her being grounded.

"Come on, Ash, time to get up," Caroline called as she threw back her covers and reached for her robe.

Ashleigh slowly rolled out of bed and grabbed her jeans and a sweatshirt. She had already missed feeding time, and didn't feel much like eating breakfast. Maybe she would just go down to the barn to spend a few extra minutes with Stardust.

The sun was shining when Ashleigh stepped from the house. Just her luck—it was going to be a beautiful day and she wouldn't be able to ride.

Jonas was pouring grain into the last of the feed

buckets when Ashleigh arrived at the barn. "Want some help?" she offered.

Jonas handed her one of the buckets. "I'm almost done, but I saved Stardust's for when you got here."

"Thanks, Jonas," Ashleigh said as she took the ration of grain and headed for Stardust's stall. The mare nickered eagerly and bobbed her head as Ashleigh approached.

"Hi there, girl." Ashleigh ran her hand along the mare's neck. "I've got spring break in a week, but it looks like you get to start vacation early."

Ashleigh dumped the grain into Stardust's bucket. "But don't worry. Just because I won't be able to ride for a while doesn't mean I won't come to visit you every day. I'm going to work real hard on my math. It won't be long before we'll be galloping over the fields together again."

Ashleigh glanced at her watch. She had just enough time to help Jonas put the mares out, then she'd have to get ready for school. Despite her worry over her math test, there was one bright spot in the morning. It was Friday. In just twenty-four more hours she would be on her way to Florida to see Aladdin.

"Don't worry about your math, Ash. There's nothing you can do now," Mona assured her.

Ashleigh sat beside her on the bus, staring grimly out the window. "I know, I know. At least I have Florida to look forward to."

"I wish I were going with you," Mona said wistfully.

"Except I'm not really sure if I'm going to like the Danworths or not," Ashleigh said.

Mona looked at her as though she were crazy. "They're flying you in their private jet. That sounds pretty nice, if you ask me."

Ashleigh stretched her legs and kicked the empty bus seat in front of her. "Yeah, but Mr. Danworth is the man who wouldn't buy any of our yearlings when Midnight was hurt. He wasn't very nice about it, either. Plus, they've got all that money and everything will be so fancy."

The school bus came to a stop and the kids began to pile out. "Oh, Ash," Mona said. "I'm sure you'll have a good time. Besides, it's just the thing to take your mind off not being able to ride—that is, if your test is really as bad as you say."

"Thanks for reminding me," Ashleigh grouched.

Mona gave her an apologetic smile as she stepped off the bus. "Oh, and I won't be in math today—I have to do the school hearing test that period. Do you think you could pick up my test for me?"

"Sure," Ashleigh said.

Mona patted her on the back. "Thanks. I'll see you

on the bus. And don't worry, Ash. Maybe you didn't do as badly as you think," she said.

"See you later," Ashleigh called, dragging her feet as they headed for their separate homerooms. She hoped the day would go slowly. She knew her math test was a total bomb, and she wasn't looking forward to the disappointment on her parents' faces when they saw her grade.

All too soon for Ashleigh, the school day was over and she was boarding the bus for home, her disastrous math test scrunched in her hand.

"Well, let's see it," Mona said, and flopped down in the bus seat next to her.

Ashleigh frowned and handed Mona her test. "You got an A," she said. "I failed." She turned to stare miserably out the bus window.

"Oh, no!" Mona exclaimed when she saw Ashleigh's grade: F. She stuffed her own test into her bag. "I'm really sorry, Ash. Let's just hope your parents go easy on you this time."

Ashleigh heard the sincerity in Mona's voice. "Thanks," she said, glancing at her friend.

Just then their friends Jamie and Lynne passed by the bus and knocked on the window.

Jamie tossed her long blond hair, grinning up at them. "Are you guys riding today?" she asked.

Ashleigh gave Mona a stricken look, and Mona pulled the bus window down. "Ashleigh flunked her math test. Her parents said that if she failed, she wouldn't be able to ride until she does better."

"Oh," the girls said in unison.

"Bummer," Lynne added.

"I'm really sorry, Ash," Jamie said. "That's the worst."

"Maybe we can do a big study session and all of us can help you," Lynne suggested.

Mona laughed. "Lynne, your math grade is almost as bad as Ashleigh's."

Lynne wadded up a piece of paper and tossed it through the open window. It bounced off Mona and hit Ashleigh in the forehead. "I know that," she said with a laugh. "But at least I'm willing to help!"

Seeing how much her friends cared made Ashleigh feel a lot better. "Thanks, guys. Spring break is coming up and I'll probably be grounded the whole time, but if we study together a little bit, I might be able to get my grade up afterward."

"It's a deal," the girls agreed.

"See you Monday," Jamie called as they waved goodbye.

The bus started, and Ashleigh spent the rest of the ride home talking about Stardust and Aladdin. When they came to her stop, she said goodbye to Mona, promising to call her as soon as they returned from Florida.

Ashleigh headed into the house, deciding it was best to avoid the barn for the moment. Her parents were probably in there, mucking out stalls and watering, and although she wanted to see Stardust, she didn't want to give her parents the bad news until she absolutely had to.

Dropping her book bag on the kitchen table, Ashleigh opened the refrigerator door and reached for a cold piece of chicken. *Might as well face the firing squad on a full stomach*, she thought with a sigh. But she had no one to blame but herself. Why hadn't she studied harder when she'd known all along this would happen?

"Is that you, girls?" Mrs. Griffen poked her head in the kitchen door.

Ashleigh's heart dropped into her stomach. "It's just me, Mom. I think I heard Caroline upstairs." Ashleigh poured herself a glass of milk and sat down at the table, feeling queasy but picking at the chicken, just to have something to do.

Mrs. Griffen walked into the room. "Don't fill up before dinner," she warned, turning on the tap to rinse off her hands. "How'd school go today? Did you get that test back?"

Ashleigh felt as if she had swallowed a chicken

bone and it was sitting sideways in her throat. "Not so good," she admitted. Her mother whirled around, and Ashleigh handed over her math test, waiting for the lecture that was sure to ensue.

Mrs. Griffen flipped through the pages with a frown. Then she set the test on the table and pulled up a chair next to Ashleigh.

"Your father and I had hoped for an improvement. Any improvement would have done. I'm really sorry, Ashleigh," she said as she brushed a lock of hair from Ashleigh's eyes.

"A horse is a big responsibility, but you also have a duty to yourself and your family. You can't just let those things slide," Mrs. Griffen went on. "We made a deal, and you haven't kept your end of the bargain. So now we've got to keep ours. I know this is going to be really tough on you, but we're going to restrict you from riding altogether until your math grade improves." She patted Ashleigh's shoulder in sympathy and stood up from the table. "I'll go break the news to your father."

The lump that felt like a chicken bone stuck further down Ashleigh's throat, threatening to gag her. No riding for what could be a long, long time. What if she *never* got better at math? She might not be able to ride for the rest of her life.

Her appetite gone, Ashleigh put the rest of the

chicken back in the refrigerator. From the kitchen window, she could see her mother and father talking in the stable yard. Her father shook his head in dismay and headed back into the barn.

Ashleigh felt a hot prickling behind her eyes. It was bad enough that she couldn't ride her horse, but she also felt bad about letting her parents down. She brushed the sleeve of her sweatshirt across her eyes and willed the tears to go away.

She grabbed her coat from the peg. She owed her parents and Stardust an apology.

As soon as she entered the barn Stardust nickered, making her feel worse than ever. "Ashleigh?" her father called from down the aisle. Ashleigh stepped to the mare's stall and stroked her soft muzzle. Then she took a deep breath and walked toward her father.

She stared at the floor, scuffing the toe of her boot on the cement and trying to keep from bursting into tears.

Mr. Griffen leaned his pitchfork against the wall and put his arm around his daughter.

"Well, we're pretty disappointed in your performance, and we *are* going to stick to what we said before: no riding until that grade comes up. That doesn't mean you're not still a regular part of this family." He squeezed her shoulder. "We've got a little while before dinner. Why don't you go pack for the trip? You can do your stalls when you're finished. We've got to get up at the crack of dawn tomorrow. You wouldn't want to miss the big race, would you?"

"No way, José!" she cried. She rushed down the aisle to give Stardust one more pat and then flew out of the barn and up to the house.

Caroline jumped when Ashleigh flew into their room. "Are you trying to give me a heart attack?" she demanded.

"We could only be so lucky," Ashleigh teased as she dragged her suitcase out from under the bed. She opened the zipper and flopped it onto the covers, then rummaged through her drawers, throwing a clean pair of jeans, a pair of sneakers, and a T-shirt into the bag. "There, all done," she sighed, zipping the suitcase.

Caroline looked at her in disbelief. "You can't possibly be done," she stated.

"I zipped the zipper," Ashleigh replied, and patted the bag. "That means I'm done. It doesn't take all day to pack for one night."

Caroline rolled her eyes and continued her own packing. "Suit yourself," she said.

Ashleigh went down to help her mother set the dinner table, then rushed out to clean her stalls and groom Stardust one last time before the trip.

Thoughts of math were already behind her—in a little over twelve more hours, she'd be on her way to see Aladdin!

"Come on, Caro. It's time to get up." Ashleigh flogged her sister with a pillow just to make sure she was awake, and smirked at the grunted response. Then she ran downstairs to put on her boots and head for the barn.

"Mornin'," Jonas called as Ashleigh walked down the aisle. "I've been expecting you." He took off his hat and scratched his gray head. "I know you don't have time to help with the feeding this morning, but I'm sure you'll want to say goodbye to Stardust. Here are some carrots," he said, handing them over with a smile.

"Thanks, Jonas," Ashleigh replied. She broke the carrots and fed them to Stardust, a piece at a time. When the carrots were all gone, she put her arms around Stardust's neck and pressed her cheek to her soft coat, inhaling the warm horse scent.

"I'm really going to miss you," Ashleigh sighed. "I don't want to leave you, but it's important that I go. One of Edgardale's horses is in trouble. Maybe I can help figure out what is wrong with him."

Stardust bobbed her head as if she understood what Ashleigh was saying.

Ashleigh rubbed the mare's forehead. "Thanks, girl. I knew you'd understand." She gave her one last hug, then ran back to the house for breakfast.

Mr. Griffen was pulling on his coat just as she came in the door. "I want to check in with Jonas before we go. I'll be gone for about ten minutes. I want everyone ready to leave by the time I get back. Anybody who's late is going to get left behind," he teased as he pulled on his gloves and walked out the door.

Like horses coming out of the starting gate, everyone shot out of their chairs and raced for their bedrooms.

"That's not fair!" Rory screamed. "You guys have longer legs than me. I can't go as fast as you!"

"Come on, I'll give you a lift," Ashleigh said, and squatted down so Rory could climb onto her back. "Up we go." She deposited him in his room, and then ran to change her clothes.

"Oh, no, you don't." Caroline pointed to the jeans that Ashleigh was about to put on. "Mom wants us to look our best. That means a dress, not jeans." She handed a blue dress to Ashleigh. "This should do. We're representing Edgardale and we need to look nice."

Ashleigh frowned. She hated wearing dresses, but she knew her sister was right. She snagged the dress from Caroline's hands. "All right," she moaned.

"Here. These shoes will go with it," Caroline said,

and handed Ashleigh a pair of patent leather Mary Janes. "Sorry, but paddock boots don't go with that outfit," she giggled.

The car horn sounded. Everyone knew what that meant: In three minutes the car would be leaving. Ashleigh grabbed her suitcase and Rory's, then ran down the stairs to the front door.

When they reached the airport, they ran their carry-on luggage through the X-ray machine, then followed an airport employee out the door to where the Danworths' private jet was waiting.

"Wow!" Caroline and Rory exclaimed as they stared, mouth agape, at the sleek silver jet with a picture of a running horse painted on the side.

The captain of the plane, an older uniformed man with a ready smile, welcomed them onboard as they climbed the portable steps into the jet.

"This is really something," Mr. Griffen remarked as he took his seat and held up a gold-rimmed beverage glass that was engraved with a horse head.

Ashleigh reached for the latest issues of *The Blood Horse* and *The Thoroughbred Record* in the magazine pocket in front of her. *Good,* she thought as she flipped through the magazine pages. She could sit in the luxurious jet seat and catch up on all the new Thoroughbred information while they winged their way to Florida.

The magazines had interesting articles on races and new bits, and one on how a "shadow roll" could improve some horses' performance. She wasn't certain what a shadow roll was. She'd have to be sure to read that article.

"Everybody buckle up," Mrs. Griffen reminded them.

Ashleigh strapped herself in, butterflies of excitement flitting about in her stomach. The view outside was a blur as the jet sped down the runway and took off. As soon as the jet had leveled off, Ashleigh reached for a magazine once more.

"Dad?" Ashleigh turned to her father when she had finished the article. "Have you ever heard of a shadow roll?"

Mr. Griffen smiled. "I've never had a horse that needed one, but they are generally used when you need a horse to lower his head," he explained. "It's a big piece of fuzzy material, kind of like the ones we use to pad some of the halters with, only bigger. It goes on the noseband of the bridle."

Mrs. Griffen leaned forward, picking a bag of pretzels from the goodie stand in front of her. "It's usually used on horses that carry their head too high. If they can't see over the shadow roll, they'll lower their head."

Ashleigh buried her nose back in the magazine,

ignoring Rory and Caroline as they played a noisy game of I Spy. She was surprised when she felt the thump of the jet's tires hitting the runway in Miami. She could see palm trees out the window as they taxied up to the terminal.

"There they are." Mr. Griffen pointed through the window to the smartly dressed man, woman, and teenage boy who waited on the tarmac. The man and woman were smiling and waving, but the lanky, sandy-haired boy just stood there with a frown on his face.

"What's he got to be grumpy about?" Ashleigh mused. She looked the boy over once more, wondering if he ever rode any of his family's horses. "He doesn't look like much of a horse person."

"Good," Caroline retorted. "Not everyone has to be totally horse-crazy like you. Anyway, Mom told me his name is Peter and he's thirteen, just like me. I think he's kind of cute."

Ashleigh gathered her bag while the steps were rolled up to the jet. "You can have him. I plan to spend all my time with Aladdin, anyway."

The door to the jet opened and the Griffen family stepped into the sunlight. Caroline paused dramatically at the top of the steps, as if to make sure all eyes, especially Peter's, were on her before she gracefully floated down the stairs.

What a show-off, Ashleigh thought as she watched Peter's eyes brighten and his frown fade at the sight of her sister. Well, Caroline wasn't the only person in the Griffen family who could put on a show.

She waited for Rory to go first, then straightened her back, lifted her chin, and stepped out into the warm Florida sunshine. She took a deep breath, imagining she could already smell coconuts and orange blossoms.

Ashleigh smiled and descended the stairs. Just as she reached the last step, she felt the heel of her left shoe slip, pitching her forward. She flailed her arms for balance and managed to stay upright, but she landed with a grunt, smack on Peter Danworth's foot.

4

Ashleigh felt the heat creep up her cheeks until her face was on fire. She kept her eyes glued to the ground, too embarrassed to look at anyone. "I'm sorry," she mumbled. When she finally looked up, the first thing she saw was the smirk on Peter's face.

"Way to go," he whispered under his breath as he extended his hand to steady her.

Ashleigh pushed his hand away, trying to make her voice sound normal, even though she was cringing on the inside.

"Thank you. I can stand on my own," she said, forcing herself to give everyone a smile so they would know she was okay. Peter was still grinning. She hoped his foot hurt as much as her pride did.

"Well, I'm certainly glad to hear that," Peter remarked, and everyone laughed at his joke. He picked up Ashleigh's and Caroline's bags and began to lead the way to the car.

Ashleigh frowned as she watched Peter's retreating back. She hated being laughed at. Her parents had taught her that she should never dislike anyone, but she thought she might have to make an exception for Peter Danworth.

"Are you okay, Ash?" Rory asked, tugging at the sleeve of her dress.

Ashleigh ruffled his hair. "I'm fine, Rory. Thanks for asking," she said as they fell into step behind the rest of the group.

Caroline slowed down until she was beside her younger sister. "Oh, Ash, how could you embarrass yourself like that?" she whispered. "We're trying to make a good impression here!"

"Well, I didn't exactly do it on purpose," Ashleigh said. "I'm not used to wearing these stupid shoes."

"Here we are," Mr. Danworth said, opening the door of a black limousine while the chauffeur hopped out to put the luggage in the trunk.

"We're certainly riding in style today," Mr. Griffen remarked, raising his eyebrows.

"Is this really your car?" Caroline asked as she stepped into the limo after her mother.

Peter scooted in behind her. "No, we just rent this when we have guests. Our family car is a BMW," he replied.

Ashleigh had just enough room to squeeze into the

backward-riding seat between the door and her mother, facing Peter and Caroline. She marveled at the fully stocked bar of sodas and the sunroof that was opened to the crystalline blue sky overhead.

"Our car is a BMW," she mimicked toward the window, but stopped short when she caught her mother's warning look.

"We're going straight to the racetrack," Mrs. Danworth said. "We shipped Aladdin in from the farm yesterday. We've got a couple of hours before the race, but my husband likes to get there in plenty of time to fuss over the horse while the grooms are getting him ready. That'll give you kids a chance to explore—maybe get a bite to eat."

Ashleigh brightened. "Can we go on the backside with you, Mr. Danworth? I can't wait to see Aladdin."

Mr. Griffen smiled. "Ashleigh helped us pick the mate for Aladdin's dam. Studied the charts to find just the right match. She's always had a special interest in that colt."

Peter frowned. "Well, she picked the wrong match. That colt sure doesn't run," he scoffed.

"Now, Peter," Mrs. Danworth cautioned. "It's still early in his career. Aladdin has only had a few starts."

"Yeah, and he's been beaten badly every time," Peter insisted. "I hear the other trainers talking. I don't like hearing other people say bad things about our horses.

They say he shouldn't even be in this race today. He's outclassed."

Ashleigh felt her face grow hot. What did he mean, *other people*? Peter himself was saying bad things about the horse. Besides, Aladdin had top-class bloodlines. He was Wanderer's Quest's half-brother, and she had been winning lots of races. He was *not* outclassed. It was on the tip of her tongue to say so when she caught a warning look from Caroline.

Caroline leaned forward to whisper in her ear. "Let it go, Ash."

But it's Peter who's being rude, Ashleigh thought to herself. He was ashamed of Aladdin and he was being nice to everyone but her. All she had done was accidentally step on his foot. That wasn't a very good reason to be mean to a person. She sighed. This was going to be a very long day.

After a short drive the limo pulled into the parking lot of the Hialeah racetrack. It was only the parking lot, but Ashleigh could tell it was a first-rate place. From where they were parked, she could see the lake on the inside of the dirt and turf tracks and the well-kept grounds with flowers in bloom.

"Look at those big pink birds!" Rory shouted, pointing at the lake.

Mrs. Danworth smiled. "Those are flamingos," she explained. "Their feathers have that pink color because of all the shrimp they eat. If they don't get shrimp, their feathers turn brown. There are lots of flamingos on the inside—they're a special attraction at this racetrack."

"I like shrimp," Rory said. "How come I'm not pink?"

Everyone laughed, including Ashleigh. Rory could be so funny sometimes.

"Hialeah has a carousel, too," Mr. Danworth said. "See it over there? Maybe you'll have time to ride it after the race."

Ashleigh would have loved to ride the beautifully painted horses on the carnival carousel, but they couldn't compare to having your very own horse. She stared out the window, wondering for a moment what Stardust was doing just then.

The limo driver opened the car doors. "We can all get out here," Mr. Danworth instructed. "Derek, if you wouldn't mind coming with me to the backside, I'd like to talk to you about some ideas I have for putting in a new broodmare barn."

Ashleigh gave her father a pleading look. She had to see Aladdin now. She couldn't wait until the race.

"Is it okay if Ashleigh comes with us?" Mr. Griffen asked. "I think she'll burst if she doesn't get to see that colt soon."

"Sure," Mr. Danworth agreed. "Peter can stay on the

51

front side and show everyone else around. Since he's not looking forward to today's race, he might be happier doing that," Mr. Danworth added, frowning at his son.

Ashleigh saw the angry look that flashed across Peter's face. *Why doesn't he like Aladdin?* she wondered. If Aladdin were her horse, she'd spend every waking moment with him. As the limo pulled away, Ashleigh had a nearly irresistible urge to stick her tongue out at it, but she managed to keep herself in check. Mr. Danworth began to lead the way to the backside and Ashleigh followed. At least she could see Aladdin now without Peter.

The backside of Hialeah was neat and tidy, and full of activity when they arrived. Grooms walked to and fro, readying horses for the day's races, while trainers checked legs and shouted out orders to assistant trainers. Ashleigh could feel the hum of excitement as they walked through the security gate.

"We're the next barn over," Mr. Danworth directed them.

Ashleigh saw the black head with the white blaze as soon as she rounded the corner. Aladdin nickered to her, bobbing his head as she approached. "Do you remember me, boy?" she called, and extended her hand to stroke his muzzle.

Derek Griffen stood outside the stall. "Looks like he's grown. Can I see him out of the stall?"

"Sure," Mr. Danworth said, and motioned for a groom to bring the colt out. "We've got to put him in crossties to get him ready. If Ashleigh will grab that box of brushes just inside the tack room, our groom probably wouldn't mind a little help. Mike Smith should be here soon—he's our new trainer."

When the groom led Aladdin out of his stall, there were several murmurs of approval up and down the shed row. The colt stood almost seventeen hands tall and was jet black with four white socks and a star and stripe. He was a stunning sight to behold.

Aladdin had been one of Edgardale's prize yearlings, and he'd been bought for a lot of money. Ashleigh was glad that high-class racing people had bought the colt—it meant that he would get the best care possible. But she wasn't sure if she liked the Danworths owning him. It still smarted that they had turned down all of Edgardale's yearling crop that year.

Ashleigh picked up the rubber currycomb and rubbed it over Aladdin's coat in a circular motion. *What are the Danworths doing wrong?* she wondered. Aladdin was bred to win. She couldn't understand how he could be losing his races by so many lengths.

As Ashleigh smoothed the currycomb over Aladdin's back, he swished his tail, gnashed his teeth, and stomped his hind legs as though he intended to kick.

"Look out!" Mr. Danworth shouted, rushing over to pull Ashleigh away.

"It's okay," Ashleigh assured him. "This is a game we used to play. He acts like he's being tickled, and he threatens to get me, but he never does. He's never hurt me. It's all an act."

"Well, I'll be." Mr. Danworth looked on in surprise as Ashleigh went to Aladdin's head and the horse nuzzled her cheek. "She's certainly got a way with horses, doesn't she?"

"I want to be a jockey someday," Ashleigh announced, moving to Aladdin's other side.

"Yes, your father has told me that. I'm sure you'll be a good one. The horses really take to you." Mr. Danworth stood at Aladdin's head while the groom picked out Aladdin's feet.

"Peter wants to be a jockey, too," Mr. Danworth added. "He does most of the galloping at home. But I don't know. . . ." He straightened and stretched his back. "At six feet two inches, I'm a pretty big guy, and I'm afraid Peter takes after my side of the family. It won't be too much longer before he'll be too big even to exercise-ride, let alone jockey. That doesn't sit very well with him. He'd like to make a career out of it."

Ashleigh was stunned. Peter a jockey? He acted as if he didn't even like horses!

"Peter has been working with some jockeys from

around here," Mr. Danworth said. "Maybe you could come watch him gallop tomorrow morning before you leave. And we've got some nice Thoroughbred hunters if you'd like to go for a ride," Mr. Danworth added.

Ashleigh looked at her dad with pleading eyes.

"Sorry, Ashleigh, but our agreement doesn't just end with Stardust, it goes for all horses," he said firmly, and turned to their host. "It's a very kind offer, but maybe some other time. Ashleigh's been having problems with her math. She's not allowed to ride for a while, until her grade improves."

"Math, you say?" Mr. Danworth handed Ashleigh the stiff body brush while he grabbed a tail comb for the groom. "Peter takes honors math. If you're having problems, I'm sure he could help."

"Thanks. I'll think about it," Ashleigh said, knowing full well that the last thing she wanted to do was be stuck with a snobby boy who would lecture her on a subject she hated.

Ashleigh finished combing Aladdin's tail. All he needed now was a quick going-over with a rub rag right before the race. She stepped back to admire their handiwork. "He's beautiful!"

Ashleigh's smile was quickly followed by a frown. Peter should have been here. He had a horse running in a stakes race that day. This was no minor event, but a grade-one stakes with a large purse. The kid had to have rocks in his head not to be even a little bit excited.

"Let's give him a couple of swallows of water, then we'll put the muzzle on him so he can't eat any more," Mr. Danworth said. "We don't want him filling up on hay—it'll slow him down. We'll wrap his legs and tack him up for the race in about an hour, so let's go over to the track kitchen and grab something cold to drink while we can."

Ashleigh had a difficult time keeping still in the track's cafeteria. There were all those beautiful horses out there being prepared for races, and she was trapped inside until Mr. Danworth thought it was time to get Aladdin ready for the race.

"Can I walk around and look at the win photos on the walls?" she asked her father.

"Sure, Ash." Mr. Griffen handed her a couple of dollars. "They're selling racing forms at the counter, too. Will you buy us one?"

Ashleigh grabbed the money and ran to the counter, anxious to see if any of the handicappers had picked Aladdin to win the race. She sat down at the nearest empty table to spread out the paper and frowned at what she saw. Nobody favored Aladdin for this race. Ashleigh folded the paper and stuffed it in her pocket. Then she stood up to examine the win photos on the walls, but she couldn't stop wondering about Aladdin. Something wasn't right—she knew he could run better.

"Let's go get Aladdin, Ashleigh," Mr. Griffen called, interrupting her thoughts. "It's almost race time."

Mike Smith, Danworth Farm's new trainer, was a burly man with a rough voice, but his eyes twinkled when he smiled. Ashleigh liked him immediately.

"What's our strategy for today, Mike?" Mr. Danworth asked him when they arrived at Aladdin's stall.

Mike grabbed several rolls of red Vetwrap and began winding the elastic bandage around Aladdin's right front leg. "We got permission from the stewards to run him in blinkers this time." He was silent for a moment while he finished the leg, then moved on to the left one. "I'm going to send him out on the engine and hope he stays there."

Out on the engine? It was all Ashleigh could do to keep her mouth shut. She might not know everything about racing, but she did know that Aladdin was from a long line of come-from-behind winners. Why would Mike send him out to the front of the pack? She looked at her father and saw that he was frowning.

Ashleigh was about to say something when her

father gave her a look that said she should keep quiet. Ashleigh sighed. What did she know, anyway? She was only ten; she had never trained a racehorse before. Mike obviously knew what he was doing.

The final call for the race was given. The trainer pulled Aladdin's racing bridle off its peg. It was white leather with a snaffle bit, and it looked great against his shiny black coat. Aladdin was guaranteed to be the best-looking horse in the race, but Ashleigh hoped he would be the fastest, too.

Mike handed the colt off to the pony horse, and they followed the horses to the paddock. Aladdin held his head high and pranced all the way.

"You're going to win," Ashleigh whispered when they parted at the paddock entrance. "I know you can." She squeezed through the throngs of people to get a better view of the horses.

"Don't wander off, Ashleigh," Mr. Griffen warned. "We're going to watch the race from the Danworths' table in the Turf Club. As soon as Aladdin starts in the post parade, we're going upstairs to sit with the rest of the gang."

Darn. Ashleigh liked to watch the races down by the rail, where you could feel the earth shake as the horses thundered down the home stretch. It was always so stuffy in the clubhouse, and it was a beautiful day. If only they could stay out in the sun.

Ashleigh looked over the rest of the horses in the race. They were impressive, and Aladdin would have his work cut out for him, especially if he was to stay in front from the start. She could only hope the blinkers would do the trick.

The bugle sounded, calling the horses to the post parade, and each horse was led out according to its post position. Aladdin had drawn the three hole, so he was one of the first to leave. Mike gave the jockey a leg up, then led the horse out to the awaiting pony.

As Mr. Danworth signed them all into the Turf Club, Ashleigh had to admit she was impressed with the fancy decor and television sets, but she would have been more impressed with a front-row spot on the fence, right at the finish line.

Ashleigh looked at Caroline, who was giggling and enjoying the lavish surroundings. Even from this far away, Ashleigh could tell her sister was fawning over Peter.

"Oh, brother!" she sighed, rolling her eyes.

"Look, Ashleigh," Rory crowed in delight. "They serve soda with little umbrellas in the glass. Isn't that cool?"

Ashleigh accepted her glass from her mother. "Yeah, that's pretty neat," she agreed as she looked at the odds board over the top of her glass. Peter must have been reading her mind, because it didn't take him long to comment.

"Eighty to one. The longest shot on the board. There's your champion for you," he sneered.

Ashleigh shot him a dirty look. "It's not over until they cross the finish line. It wouldn't hurt you to root for him, either," she shot back. "After all, he *is* your dad's horse."

Peter snorted. "A lot of good it would do."

"Don't be such a brat, Ash," Caroline said, defending her new friend.

Ashleigh gave her the same frown she had just given Peter. The two of them were exactly alike. They really couldn't care less about horses. Ashleigh wondered how Caroline could be so different from the rest of the family.

"They're putting them in the gate." Rory pointed. "There goes Aladdin!"

Ashleigh put her glass back on the table, afraid to hold it in her shaking hands. Aladdin just had to win this race. He had to prove Peter wrong!

"They're off!" the announcer called.

Aladdin sprang from the gate. The jockey was pushing him hard, trying to get to the front of the pack before the first turn. He slipped past the inside horses and was running easily on the inside rail, his big stride carrying him around the turn.

"And it's Aladdin on the inside rail with Jump Up Johnny running second and Let's Tango hanging in for third as they head down the stretch and into the first turn," the announcer said.

"Go, Aladdin, go!" Ashleigh jumped to her feet to yell with the rest of the crowd.

"He's going to fade," Peter predicted. "Look at the fractions he's setting. He can't keep that up for a mile and an eighth."

Ashleigh spun on her heels. She knew the pace was grueling, and Peter might be right, but she wasn't about to admit it. "Yes, he will. You just watch!" she challenged.

At the half-mile and three-quarter-mile poles, Aladdin was still holding on. Ashleigh saw the hope creep into Peter's face.

"It's Aladdin running handily, with Let's Tango in second. Jump Up Johnny is fading, and Misty Aisle is coming on strong to challenge the leaders!" the announcer called.

"Come on, boy," Peter whispered under his breath.

Misty Aisle moved up alongside Aladdin, but Aladdin held on to his lead.

Peter jumped up next to Ashleigh. "Come on!" he yelled. "You can do it! Come on, Aladdin!"

Ashleigh gave him a big smile, and Peter grinned back. Maybe he wasn't as bad as she had thought.

Coming out of the turn, the jockey laid on the whip and the big black horse began to falter, his great, graceful gallop switching visibly to an awkward, gangly lope. The outside horses caught up to him and began to pass. Aladdin pinned his ears, raised his head, and increased his pace, making a valiant attempt to maintain the lead, but the early fast fractions had taken their toll. Little by little, he slipped farther and farther toward the back of the pack.

"Aladdin is losing ground, and Misty Aisle is moving up to take the lead," the announcer called.

"What happened?" Peter sputtered. "Let's go, Big Al—hang on!" But it was no use. Aladdin was sFalling behind.

Ashleigh looked at Peter. *Big Al?* she wondered. *He must really care about Aladdin after all if he has a pet name for him.*

"Misty Aisle wins by two lengths, with Let's Tango hanging on for second and Another Joker placing third," the man announced the final call.

Peter flopped back down in his chair, disappointment etched into his features. Ashleigh felt as bad as Peter looked. What *had* happened? Aladdin had been running fine until the stretch, when the rider used his whip. She knew some horses were whip-shy. Was it the fast fractions or the whip that had cost Aladdin the race?

"It's like he hit a brick wall," Peter said. "I knew it was too good to be true. He's just a cheap claimer. He's got no business running with this class of horses." He folded his arms, and the frown settled on his brow once again.

Mr. Danworth sighed heavily. "I guess you'd better look this over." He shoved a sheet of paper over the table to Ashleigh's father.

"What's this?" Mr. Griffen picked up the paper and studied it.

"It's our legal agreement to send Aladdin to Edgardale to stand at stud."

Ashleigh's heart leaped for joy. But her happiness was marred by the quick flash of despair that passed over Peter's face.

"Let's not be too hasty," Derek Griffen said, and set the paper back on the table.

Mr. Danworth grabbed his racing form and stood up. "Derek, we've talked about this for weeks now. This is not a hasty decision. My wife and I feel we've given the colt plenty of time, and he's just not working out the way we had hoped," he said, shaking his head.

"You can say that again," Peter interrupted. "And he was an expensive mistake." He turned to face Ashleigh. "You like him so much, it looks like you've got him. I hope you have a great time with *my horse!*"

Peter stood up so fast, his chair tipped over. Without a backward glance, he tore off down the stairs.

Caroline looked as if she wanted to go after him, but she stayed where she was, watching Peter run away.

Mrs. Griffen picked up the chair. "Will he be all right?" she asked the Danworths.

"Peter's going through a rough time right now," Mrs. Danworth said. "Aladdin *is* his horse, and he had high hopes for him."

Rory slurped the rest of his soda, his eyes following Peter's descent down the stairs. "He looks pretty sad," he noted.

Ashleigh could have sworn Peter had tears in his eyes. Why would he cry if he disliked Aladdin? She stared back and forth between her father and Mr. Danworth. "*His* horse?" she asked.

Mr. Danworth nodded. "We gave Aladdin to Peter for his twelfth birthday." When he saw Ashleigh's eyebrows rise, he continued.

"I know that seems like an awfully pricey birthday gift, but the horse is still under my control as far as training and caring for him are concerned."

Ashleigh felt as though she was being pulled in two different directions. She desperately wanted Aladdin to come home to Edgardale. A lot of their mares would be perfect crosses for him. And it would be a great opportunity for her father to expand his breeding business by catering to outside clients. But at the same time a little voice inside her wouldn't let her forget that Aladdin should be a champion. To retire him now would mean that he would forever be known as the horse that couldn't even place in a race. He might have great bloodlines, but a lot of broodmare owners would pass him up because he had never proven himself at the track.

Then Peter's face, with its betrayed expression, came back to haunt her. He had been so hopeful when Aladdin looked as though he might win the race. And he had looked so miserable when he knew he was about to lose his horse.

Ashleigh didn't know if she should mention her suspicion that Aladdin was whip-shy. No one had asked for her opinion, but she had to do something to salvage Aladdin's racing career. She couldn't just keep her mouth shut. Aladdin needed to prove himself. He could do that only if he was allowed to race.

"Can't you give Aladdin a couple more chances?" Ashleigh pleaded. "I *know* he can be a champion!" She lowered her eyes to the table, feeling very small under the weight of everyone's stares.

Mrs. Griffen put a comforting hand on Ashleigh's shoulder.

Mr. Griffen nodded. "As much as I'd like to have

that colt in my barn, I think I have to side with Ashleigh. Aladdin's had only five starts. He showed moments of greatness today. Why don't we try to figure out what it takes to make him run before you give up completely?" he said.

Mr. Danworth tipped his hat and scratched his head. "We've been trying. I'm at my wits' end. Maybe you could suggest something?" he asked.

"I don't know." Mr. Griffen turned his eyes to his wife. "We'd have to be around the colt, study him. That's kind of difficult to do from Kentucky."

"Well, Peter's spring break is only a week away," Mrs. Danworth said. "Your kids must have a break soon, too. How would you and your family like to join us for their break? We've got a swimming pool and a lake for fishing," she said, looking at Rory, Caroline, and Ashleigh.

"All right!" Rory piped up, turning his big blue eyes to his mother. "Can we stay, Mom? Please?"

Elaine Griffen smiled at Rory, then looked at her husband. "What do you think, Derek? Can we get away from the farm for a week? Foaling time starts soon, remember," she reminded him.

Mr. Griffen stroked his chin, seeming to weigh the decision. "We have only one mare due that week. I think Jonas could handle it. We could get the Worton boys to help Jonas with the stalls."

"Please, Dad," Caroline begged.

The Griffen family held their breath, waiting for his answer.

Mr. Griffen looked at his children's faces. "I'm sure none of you would mind," he said, grinning. "I say, let's do it!"

Rory and Caroline cheered.

"Then it's settled." Mr. Danworth extended his hand. "You'll spend the holiday with us, and we won't scratch Aladdin from his next race, two weeks from today."

Ashleigh let out the breath she had been holding. She wasn't sure if she was happy or not. A whole week without seeing Stardust would be hard, and so would a week with Peter. But seven days on a big training farm full of amazing racehorses, *and* with a pool and a fishing pond, would be heaven. She might even be able to figure out why Aladdin wasn't running right.

Mr. Griffen pushed the contract back across the table. "You hang on to this." He placed his hat on his head and extended his hand to Mr. Danworth. "It's all settled, then. We'll have a week to pick apart everything that colt does. Maybe between us we'll be able to figure something out." He tweaked a lock of Ashleigh's hair. "And maybe Ashleigh can work on her math with Peter, so that she can ride again when she gets back."

Ashleigh tried a convincing smile, then turned back

to the racetrack, looking over the next batch of horses entering the paddock area. Out of the corner of her eye she caught a glimpse of the big black colt with the four white socks. Behind him, Peter walked with a dejected set to his shoulders.

Ashleigh sighed. Spending a week at the Danworths' could be fun, but what about Peter? Could she stand a whole week of his mood swings? She'd have to count on her sister to keep him occupied most of the time so that she could have full run of the barn and do as little math as possible.

5

"A WHOLE WEEK IN FLORIDA! I AM SO JEALOUS!" JAMIE SAID as they walked out the school door together.

"Yeah, you'll come back with a tan and everything." Lynne said, pulling her blond hair back into a ponytail.

Ashleigh hefted her book bag onto her shoulder. "The only bad thing is that I'll be staying on a farm that has lots of horses, and I won't be able to ride any of them. It's going to be like torture!"

"That's too bad," Mona sympathized. "But look at the bright side. If Peter tutors you in math, you might be able to get your riding privileges back by the end of spring break."

Ashleigh smiled. She hadn't thought about that. She stopped outside their bus. "The Danworths have some really nice hunters. If I weren't grounded, I could spend all my time there riding."

69

Mona sighed. "Oh, but Ashleigh, think of all the wonderful racehorses you're going to be around. And the pool. Don't the Danworths live close to the beach, too?" she asked.

"Yeah," Ashleigh said. "Wouldn't it be fun to ride horses on the beach?"

They all took a moment to imagine it.

"Let's go. The bus is leaving," the driver called out to them.

Ashleigh stepped onto the bus and threw her book bag under the seat in front of her. *Horses on the beach,* she mused, and kept that daydream in her head all the way home.

Two days before they were supposed to leave for Florida, Jonas slipped and fell while moving hay from the loft and had to spend the night in the hospital.

Ashleigh had been down in the aisle, helping with the morning feed, when he fell. Jonas had gotten to his feet and dusted himself off, saying he was fine, but her parents were worried and insisted that they take him to the doctor. It was a good thing they did. Jonas had a concussion. The doctors wanted to keep him overnight for observation.

Ashleigh didn't mind doing Jonas's chores. The extra work meant she could stay in the barn longer and spend more time with Stardust. It really hurt, not being able to ride. But Ashleigh had been making up for it by spending more time grooming her and doing ground work. She talked to the mare constantly while they worked, telling her all about Aladdin and how they had to find out what was making him run so badly.

When she came home from school that afternoon, Ashleigh pulled on her gloves and grabbed the wheelbarrow and mucking tools. Her breath came out in clouds as she pushed the wheelbarrow down the aisle to Stardust's stall. She looked out the window at the low clouds in the sky. It definitely wasn't like Florida. Her mother said that a freak cold front was moving into the area and might even bring snow.

Ashleigh finished the stall and went to get Go Gen. The gray mare still hadn't foaled—she was almost a week overdue and her belly was immense. Ashleigh had seen the uneasy look in her parents' eyes when they handled Go Gen. She hoped the mare foaled before they left for Florida. And when she did, her foal would be a full brother or sister to Aladdin.

Ashleigh finished mucking out Go Gen's stall and dumped the contents of the wheelbarrow. The sky was growing dark and a few snowflakes drifted down, landing softly on the freezing ground.

Ashleigh blew into her gloves. She wished the

weather would change. It was better to have warm weather for the coming foals.

She smiled as she watched Stardust trot across the paddock with her neck arched and her tail in the air. The mare snorted and her breath came out in frozen plumes. *If only I could ride,* Ashleigh thought.

Ashleigh put the rake and wheelbarrow back in their place. She had just enough time to put the mares in before dinner. She had to study her math that night. Her teacher had threatened to give them a pop quiz before spring break.

Ashleigh entered the house, pulling off her mittens and coat. Prince Charming greeted her at the door, winding around her ankles and purring. "You're not making it very easy to take my boots off," she admonished the cat before picking him up and scratching him under the chin.

Rory appeared around the corner. "Dinner's ready," he said as he took the kitten from her so she could take off her boots.

"What are we having?" Ashleigh flexed her fingers to shake off the cold.

"Pizza!" Rory exclaimed. "Mom and Caroline made homemade pizza. They let me put the pepperoni on."

Ashleigh's stomach gurgled, and she laughed. "I guess that means it's time to eat." She followed Rory into the dining room. Her mom was just setting the pizza on the table, but her father wasn't in his chair.

"Everyone dig in," Mrs. Griffen said. "Your father called to say he was on his way home from the feed store, and not to wait for him."

Ashleigh pulled a piece from the pie, the cheese stretching all the way to her plate. Doing all the extra barn work had given her a huge appetite.

They heard the front door open. A moment later Mr. Griffen stepped into the room, his jacket dusted with a light coating of snow.

"Wow," Caroline said as she put a helping of pizza on their father's plate. "Looks like the weatherman was right. We've got snow."

Mr. Griffen took off his jacket and hung it close to the heater to dry. "Yes. It's supposed to blow through tonight, then start warming up. I don't relish the thought of standing foal watch tonight in a snow-storm." He took a big bite of pizza.

The phone sounded, ringing loud and clear among their chatter. Mrs. Griffen answered it.

"Oh, no!" she murmured after listening to the voice on the other end. "Uh-huh . . . I see. We'll be right there." She hung up and reached for the car keys. "Put your jacket back on, Derek. The cold weather has busted a big pipe in the Wortons' broodmare barn. They've got mares and foals standing ankle deep in freezing water, and they need our help."

Mr. Griffen grabbed another piece of pizza and slipped into his jacket. "You guys clean up after dinner and do your homework. We'll be home as soon as we can."

"Can I come?" Ashleigh rose from her chair. The thought of all those mares with their new foals standing in the freezing water made her sick at heart. They had to get them someplace warm and dry before they caught pneumonia.

Mr. Griffen put on his hat and gloves. "No, Ashleigh. Go Gen could go anytime now. We'll only be gone a few hours. I need you to keep an eye on that mare."

"But don't forget—you've got another math test coming up. You'd better study, too," her mother reminded her.

Mrs. Griffen zipped up her coat and kissed each of them on top of the head. "We'll call as soon as things are under control. Caroline, you're in charge. We should be home in about two hours. You have the Wortons' number if you need us."

Ashleigh walked them to the door and waved goodbye. It was snowing much harder now. Fat flakes fell to the ground and were blown across the yard by a sharp, freezing wind. Ashleigh closed the door, shivering in her thin sweatshirt.

As soon as the car engine started and the crunch of

tires on gravel receded into the distance, Caroline popped out of her chair and headed for the stairs.

"It's your turn to do the dishes, Ashleigh. Rory can help you so you can get down to the barn. I'm going to pick out my wardrobe for this weekend," she announced, then turned and sprinted up the stairs.

Ashleigh frowned. "What's the big deal?" She was excited about seeing Aladdin again, but she wasn't so sure about everything that went along with it. She had reservations about spending a whole week in a fancy house with carpet so clean, you weren't allowed to step on it in your shoes.

She picked up the dirty dishes and stacked them by the sink, staring dreamily out the window at the snow gathering on the lawn. What would it be like to own a farm like the Danworths', where they trained their own horses? They seemed to be very successful. Maybe when they were down there some of it would rub off on her father, and he'd agree to build a training track at Edgardale.

Ashleigh finished the dishes and checked on Rory. He had busied himself with the TV and was now lying half asleep on the floor. She'd let him doze a while longer while she made some peanut butter sandwiches for her father to eat during foal watch when he got back.

Ashleigh paused when the lights flickered. She heard the television make a crackling sound. "What was that?" Rory said, coming into the kitchen and rubbing his eyes.

"Looks like the storm is getting worse," Ashleigh said with a shiver. She filled a thermos with hot chocolate, put the sandwiches in plastic bags, and threw everything into a sack. She hoped the lights didn't go out—that was always scary. And she hoped her parents wouldn't be gone long.

Ashleigh wiped her hands on her jeans, picked up her math book, and headed for the living room. Rory was back on the couch, half asleep, half watching the television. "Rory, wake up, it's time to go to bed," Ashleigh called. Rory yawned, mumbled something impossible to discern, and headed up the stairs.

Ashleigh made herself comfortable on the couch, opened her math book, and began to work out the problems. A few moments later a soft tapping sound drew Ashleigh's attention to the window. The wind gusted, blowing hundreds of tiny particles of crusted snow against the pane. Ashleigh frowned as her mind began to wander to the barn. The storm was moving in quickly. It was a good thing the tack room in the barn was heated. Her father was in for a cold night on foal watch. Go Gen had started dripping milk earlier in the day. That was a good sign that it was her time. Maybe she should go check on the mare, she thought. Her parents had asked her to keep an eye on Go Gen. They wouldn't mind if she put down her math for this.

"Caro," she hollered up the stairs, "I'm heading out to the barn."

6

ASHLEIGH PULLED HER HEAVY PARKA FROM THE PEG AND put her raincoat on over it. It would keep the snow from melting into the seams of her jacket and getting it wet. Then she grabbed a pair of gloves, scooped up her father's sack of food, and headed out the door.

She wasn't prepared for the cold gust of wind that greeted her, driving the tiny particles of ice and snow against her skin. She sucked in her breath. It felt as though she were being stung by a hive of bees. She bent her head against the storm, wrapping her jackets close about her, and sprinted toward the barn.

The wind howled like a lone wolf, blowing against her in heavy gusts. The snow and ice whipped through her hair and stuck to her eyelashes. This was no kind of weather for the end of March. Where had this freak storm come from? She hoped her parents would be home soon.

Ashleigh had almost reached the barn when her feet found a slick patch of ice. She felt her boots slide on the frozen ground, and she did a dance trying to keep her balance. It was useless.

A surprised yelp escaped her lips as her arms windmilled in the air, sending the sack of food high into the sky. Her feet slipped this way and that before she finally lost the battle and crashed to the ground. The thermos smacked the ground by her feet and the sandwiches pelted her on the head.

Ashleigh sat in a daze. The fall hurt so much, she felt tears spring to her eyes, but she was too big for that. She got to her hands and knees, gathered the sandwiches and hot chocolate, and then carefully rose to her feet to open the barn door.

She tugged with all her might, but the door barely moved. Then she dropped the food and gave the door another good, hard yank. Finally it moved along its rollers, opening just wide enough for her to slip inside and close it behind her.

A volley of neighs greeted her. The barn was dark and almost silent compared to the storm that raged outside. She inhaled the welcoming smell of horses and hay.

Ashleigh slid her hand slowly along the wall, searching for the light switch, and quickly flipped it on. Light flooded the stable and she breathed a sigh of relief.

Stardust poked her elegant head over the stall door and whinnied, flipping her muzzle up and down in greeting, and the other horses followed suit. Ashleigh listened to the nervous shuffling of the mares as they paced around their stalls, nickering softly to each other.

"Easy," Ashleigh crooned as she walked down the aisle, greeting each horse. Moe poked his head over the door, looking for the carrot that Ashleigh usually offered him. "Just a minute, you chow hound. Let me get this stuff put away and take this wet coat off."

She opened the tack room door and flipped on the light, pulling the smashed sandwiches out of the wet sack and setting them on the desk beside the thermos. She slipped out of her raincoat and hung it over the heater. Fortunately, her parka was still dry.

Ashleigh checked the foaling stall next to the tack room. Go Gen stood at the back of her stall, her head lowered and one back foot cocked in the resting position. She looked miserable. The mare hadn't had much of an appetite, either—her hay net and water bucket were still full. That was a clear sign that her time was near.

"You okay?" Ashleigh spoke softly as she entered the stall. Go Gen nuzzled her face, her warm, sweet breath wafting over Ashleigh's frozen cheeks.

Ashleigh glanced around the foaling stall. It was

twice the size of a regular stall, giving the mare plenty of room to move around and give birth. The one-way window on the wall between the tack room and the foaling stall let the foaling attendant watch the process without alarming the mare. That was where Ashleigh's father would spend the night.

She removed Go Gen's halter, listening to the sound of the wind as it swept over the barn. The lights flickered again, and Ashleigh held her breath, hoping they would stay on.

After a few moments the lights were still blazing brightly, and Ashleigh heaved a sigh of relief. If there was a problem, her parents would need the light to help deliver the foal.

The shrill ring of the phone cut through the night, and Ashleigh nearly leaped out of her skin. She laughed at herself for being so jumpy, and then ran down the aisle and picked up the receiver. "Hello?"

Her sister's voice crackled over the line.

"Ash, Mom and Dad are stuck at the Wortons' place. The roads are too icy to make it home. They said they'll be here as soon as the storm breaks and the roads are safe to travel. Are you going to be okay?" her sister asked.

"Sure," Ashleigh said with a bravado she didn't feel. Already her knees were beginning to shake. What if the mare foaled that night and there was a problem?

She had seen foals born many times before, but she hadn't done more than watch. What good would she be if there was a problem?

She mustered up her courage. "I'll be okay until Mom and Dad get here. Don't worry, Caro, I'll be all right," she assured her sister.

Ashleigh said good night and hung up the phone. She tucked her hands into her pockets and listened to the storm raging outside. The wind hammered snow and ice against the window, and the lights flickered again. *What am I going to do now?*

Ashleigh sighed, wishing Jonas were there. She could have used his calm assurance and experience. If Jonas were there, it wouldn't be such a disaster that her parents were stuck at the neighboring farm. Poor Jonas. She hoped he was all right.

Tap, tap, tap. A branch fluttered against the barn window, sounding like a large bird pecking away at the sill. Ashleigh stayed where she was, crouched below the telephone, and watched while the barn lights did a flickering dance.

How long before my parents make it home? Ashleigh wondered as she considered her options. She *could* go back to the house and study her math for a while, and then just go to bed. But what if Go Gen needed her?

Go Gen's foal would be Aladdin's full brother or sister, and once they found the key to making Aladdin run, he'd be a great champion and this new foal would be worth a lot. After Midnight Wanderer's loss earlier that year, Edgardale needed a boost. Besides, Ashleigh had promised her parents she would look after the mare. She would have to stay in the barn.

Stardust nickered to her from the end of the barn. Ashleigh took a deep breath and stood, brushing the dirt from her pants. There were things to be done. She'd have to forget about math for now.

Ashleigh made her way back to the tack room and checked on the foaling kit—iodine for the umbilical cord, towels for drying off the foal, string and scissors in case the cord had to be cut, a tail wrap. Although she knew their use, she'd never used any of them herself before. But she would have to try. She took out the tail wrap and filled a coffee can full of sweet feed, carrying them back to Go Gen's stall. The mare was standing in the corner with her head down, but her ears pricked when Ashleigh shook the grain can. Finally she ambled forward with a hungry nicker.

"Guess we've got at least a few hours to go if you've still got an appetite for grain," Ashleigh said with a smile. She poured the grain into the corner feeder and waited until the mare had her nose buried deep in the bucket before beginning to braid and wrap Go Gen's long black and gray tail to keep it out of the way of the birth.

Ashleigh took off her gloves and hummed a quiet tune as she pulled one thick hank of hair over the other in a crisscross pattern. When she reached the bottom of the braid, she doubled it up and rolled the tail wrap over it, snug but not too tight. She had heard it said that if you wrapped a horse's tail too tightly, the tail would fall off. Ashleigh didn't know if that was true, but she didn't want to find out!

"There, we're done." Ashleigh stood back to admire her handiwork. It was almost as good as her father's. "But Go Gen, it would really be better if you didn't have this baby tonight," Ashleigh said as she hugged the mare. "There's nobody else here. I'm all you've got." The gray mare swished her tightly wrapped tail and turned to look at Ashleigh with soft brown eyes.

Ashleigh ran her hands through the mare's long black mane, combing it with her fingers. "I've never done this before," she explained, and patted the mare's shoulder. "Hold on. I'm going to get you something to munch on."

Ashleigh grabbed the wheelbarrow and filled it with hay. The tapping at the window had stopped, and she could no longer hear the harsh gusting of wind that drove the frozen snow against the barn's windows. Maybe the storm was letting up and her parents would make it home.

She gave each mare a flake of hay and checked to

make sure their water buckets weren't iced over. The tack room was heated, but the rest of the barn was not. She looked at her watch and yawned. It was almost eleven o'clock. Her warm bed would feel so good, but she didn't dare leave the barn. Go Gen was her responsibility now. She couldn't let anything happen to the mare or her unborn foal.

Ashleigh put the wheelbarrow back in its spot, then stopped by Stardust's stall to say good night. The chestnut mare lifted her head and nickered but stayed where she was, pulling mouthfuls of hay from the hay net.

There was a clock in the tack room. Ashleigh set it for 1 A.M. and threw a pile of horse blankets together for a bed. She would sleep for two hours. If Go Gen was going to foal that night, she'd be showing definite signs by that time. Before she went to sleep, Ashleigh checked the one-way window between the tack room and the foaling stall. If all went well with the delivery, her parents usually waited until the foal stood to nurse before they entered the stall and gave the foal its first contact with a human. If there was trouble, they would enter the stall immediately.

Go Gen paced nervously about her stall. It looked like the foal was on its way, no matter what Ashleigh had to say about it.

Ashleigh had been asleep for only an hour when a

sudden gust of wind pushed against the front of the barn, sending the large sliding door rocking on its hinges. Her head snapped up at the loud bang, and she rose from her cozy spot on the floor, pushing aside the horse blanket and going to the one-way window. Go Gen was quiet for the moment.

The wind continued its assault, sounding like the gusty blasts that came before a spring tornado. The tree branch pounded a wild beat against the side of the barn. Several of the mares nickered nervously to one another.

Ashleigh heard a high-pitched whinny and recognized Stardust's call. She opened the tack room door and went to the mare. "Easy, girl. It's just the wind," she said in a comforting tone when she reached the chestnut's stall. Stardust stuck her head over the door, pushing her soft nose into the front of Ashleigh's coat.

Ashleigh cupped the mare's muzzle in her hands. "You're in here, where it's safe and sound. Nothing's going to happen to you."

There was a moment of silence, as though the storm were holding its breath, and then the wind hammered the barn with gale force. A tree branch hit the window with a sharp crack. Ashleigh jumped and her breath caught in her throat.

The sound of shattering glass filled the barn as the broken pieces tinkled to the floor. Before she could take another breath, the lights went out, plunging the barn into total darkness.

Ashleigh stood rooted to the spot, her heartbeat hammering in her ears. She counted to ten, hoping the lights would be back on before she could finish. Several moments passed, but the barn remained cloaked in darkness.

Stardust nickered and pushed at Ashleigh's back, almost knocking her to the ground. Ashleigh regained her balance but stayed where she was, straining to see through the darkened barn. The cold wind whistled through the broken window, sending a chill across her face. She could feel cold flecks of snow blow against her cheeks.

With the electricity out, the small heater in the tack room would also be gone. The temperature in the barn was already dropping.

Ashleigh wondered if the house lights were out, too. Hands outstretched, she shuffled to the wall of the barn, then felt her way down the length of the aisle to the side window that faced the house. She peered into a night that was blacker than Aladdin's coat. Even if Caroline and Rory had gone to bed, Caro would leave a light on in the kitchen for her and their parents. There were no lights on in the house.

Ashleigh tamped down a lump of fear that rose in her throat. She would *not* panic. The lights could come back on any second now.

She stood in the aisle, her ears straining to catch every sound. She was hoping for the hum of electricity from somewhere, but the only thing she heard was the stamping of hooves and the scrape of the tree branch as it rattled against the broken window. It wasn't that she was scared. This was her barn and it was full of horses. What did she have to be afraid of? Then she remembered the phone. She would call the house and make sure everyone was okay. Maybe she could talk Caroline or Rory into coming down and staying with her.

Ashleigh sighed. Now that the lights were out, it would be too dark to see Go Gen from the one-way window in the tack room. She'd have to take her horse blanket and sit outside the stall so she could at least hear what was going on. That was what her parents and Jonas would do.

She felt better now that she had a plan. Moving back to the wall, Ashleigh made her way down the aisle, feeling for the telephone. When she found it, she lifted the receiver and dialed the house number to update Caroline. But it was no use. The phone was dead.

Ashleigh put down the receiver, wondering if she should run up to the house, just for a moment. *I could get a flashlight,* she thought. But a grunt from Go Gen's stall and the sound of the mare lying down to roll brought Ashleigh's thoughts back to the other problem at hand. The mare was going into labor. What was she going to do? She felt a tear slip down her cheek and angrily brushed it away. She had to *think*. There was no time to cry!

7

Ashleigh found her way back to the tack room and rummaged around for the flashlight., knocking over most of the things on the desk before she found it. She went to Go Gen's stall and shone the small ray of light inside. The mare was lying flat on her side, but she rose immediately when the light hit her.

Ashleigh's hand shook on the flashlight. She tried to tell herself it was just from the cold, but she knew better. She was scared. She had been around horses all her life, and she had seen several of the foals born, but being alone in a dark barn with a mare that might have problems foaling would be more than she could handle.

But she had to be sure that nothing happened to this foal. If Aladdin proved to be the champion race-horse that she knew he could be, and with Wanderer's

Quest for a half sister, Mr. Danworth would pay a lot to have this colt in his barn. This time he wouldn't look down his nose at Edgardale's horses!

Ashleigh moved the flashlight beam to the wall of the stall and quietly opened the door. "Are you okay, pretty girl?" she crooned, imitating the tone she'd often heard Jonas and her parents use with the horses.

The mare's ears pricked and she tipped her head toward Ashleigh, but she didn't move.

Ashleigh ran her hands over the mare's neck and chest. She felt warm to the touch but hadn't broken into a sweat yet. When she went into labor, her sides would be flecked with sweat.

The mare grunted again and shuffled around the stall. She lipped her hay pile but didn't seem at all interested in eating.

It wouldn't be long now. Ashleigh grabbed a pile of horse blankets from the tack room and settled in front of Go Gen's stall to wait. As she began to warm up, the comforting sound of the horses munching their hay worked their magic and Ashleigh felt her eyes growing heavy. She fought against sleep. She needed the blankets to stay warm, but she had to stay awake. Nothing could happen to this foal!

The last sound she heard before she drifted off was Stardust's soft nicker down the aisle.

• • •

Ashleigh woke with a start. How long had she been asleep? Five minutes? Three hours? She pulled the blankets off her face and was surprised by the dim light that came in from the barn windows. It was almost daybreak, and a faint predawn glow was sifting into the barn, offering just enough light for her to see.

Ashleigh lay perfectly still, listening to the sounds of the barn. All was quiet for a moment; then she heard the ragged breathing of the pregnant mare in the stall beside her. Go Gen drew in a deep breath, then exhaled with a grunt. Ashleigh could tell by the sounds that the mare was lying down in the stall and probably was in labor.

She crawled from her blanket and peeked over the stall door. The faint light from the broken window hadn't penetrated the stall. It was dark, and Ashleigh couldn't see a thing.

The mare groaned again, and Ashleigh's breath caught. She knew it was normal for a mare to be uncomfortable, but how was she supposed to tell a normal birthing groan from one that said the mare was in trouble?

Ashleigh grabbed the flashlight and let herself inside the stall. Startled by the flashlight's glare, Go Gen snorted and scrambled awkwardly to her feet, blowing through her nostrils and flicking her tail.

"Easy, girl. Everything's going to be all right. I'll be right here with you," Ashleigh called. She felt the mare's neck. It was damp with sweat. This looked like the real thing. It wouldn't be much longer. Ashleigh pulled the blankets into the stall and sat in the corner to wait.

Go Gen nipped at her sides and pawed the ground. She paced back and forth, her breathing heavy and loud.

Ashleigh shivered, unable to distinguish whether it was nerves or the freezing temperatures that were making her shake. She took a deep breath and watched the mare continue to pace.

After a few minutes passed, Ashleigh heard the noise she had been waiting for—like water spilling over the sides of a bucket. The mare's water had broken.

Ashleigh felt the blood pounding through her veins. This was it! After a mare's water broke, the foal was usually on the ground within twenty minutes. She fought the urge to pull her hands from her pockets and look at her watch. She didn't want to do anything to disturb the mare. She remembered Jonas's warning: *These mares are pretty quick. You've got about a twenty-minute window for delivery. If the foal isn't born by then, you've got problems.*

Ashleigh's legs were so numb from sitting in the same position, they felt as though they had fallen off. Still, she didn't move.

Go Gen got up and down several times. Ashleigh knew this was normal. It would help put the foal into position. As the mare grunted and groaned and strained to push the foal from her body, Ashleigh tried to remember if this was the way all the mares had delivered. Had they gotten up and down so many times? She couldn't remember the others grunting so much, but she had been in the tack room with the walls and window between them.

It seemed as though an eternity had passed. Had it been twenty minutes yet? Surely the foal should be on the ground by now. Her excitement was mixed with a good dose of worry. Go Gen was more than a week overdue. That meant an extra week of growing for the foal—what if it was too big to come out?

Ashleigh felt herself begin to shake uncontrollably. It started in her hands and worked its way up to her arms and shoulders. The muscles in her legs begged to move; her feet were asleep, and it felt as though a thousand needles were pricking her. She couldn't help it—she just had to shift her position. She tried to be quiet, but the rustle she made in the straw sounded like an elephant in a china factory.

Go Gen snorted and got to her feet, swaying

slightly as she faced Ashleigh's corner, trying to see into the darkness.

"No," Ashleigh groaned. "Don't stop, Go Gen. You've got to have this baby quickly. We're running out of time." She glanced at her watch, but it didn't do her any good. She had no idea what time the mare's water had broken.

Go Gen shuffled forward and sniffed Ashleigh, then returned to the middle of the stall and immediately lay down as another contraction overcame her.

Ashleigh noted that there seemed to be more light in the stall now. She squinted, making out the shape of the mare as she lay on her side, her legs going stiff with each contraction.

At her first glimpse of the foal's forelegs and nose, Ashleigh breathed a small sigh of relief. The baby was in the correct position. After a couple of pushes, the head, neck, and front legs were out. Then Go Gen took a moment to rest.

Ashleigh knew this was normal. The mare had to gather her strength for the next big push. This would be the hardest one. Once the foal's large shoulders were clear of the mare, the rest of the birth would happen very quickly.

Go Gen strained again, pushing with all her might, resting only a few moments before the next contraction hit. Soon the foal's shoulders appeared and were quickly followed by the rest of its body. Go Gen lay on her side resting while the foal took its first breaths and lifted its tiny head.

Ashleigh sat in the corner, straining to see. The foal's coat was wet, but it looked black. The foal shifted a bit on the straw, and Ashleigh could see that it had three white socks and a blaze—almost an exact replica of Aladdin! Rory had guessed the colt would be black—she couldn't wait to tell him the good news. Ashleigh usually named the new foals, but because of Rory's guess, he would get to name the foal this time.

Go Gen pulled her legs up close to her body and rolled up to a resting position, craning her neck to look at the new foal. She nickered softly to her baby.

Ashleigh's heart swelled as she watch the still-wet foal shake its head and blow through its nostrils before attempting to lunge to its feet. Its legs went this way and that, not quite working together, but getting more coordinated with each try.

Ashleigh got on her hands and knees and crept closer to the mare and foal. She didn't want to startle the baby or upset the mare.

On the fourth attempt, the foal managed to gain its feet for a few seconds, breaking the umbilical cord in the process. The youngster wobbled and bobbed, taking a few steps toward Ashleigh before it collapsed in a heap once more. Ashleigh could see that the foal was a filly. Aladdin and Quest had a new sister!

Ashleigh couldn't help but laugh at the bewildered look on the new filly's face. Go Gen nickered her concern and got to her feet, licking her foal's coat and gently nudging her to stand.

"Good girl," Ashleigh encouraged. "You can do it. Look how strong you are already."

The foal started at the sound of a human voice, swaying on shaky legs as she turned to face the sound.

Ashleigh held her breath as Go Gen moved forward to place herself between Ashleigh and the new filly.

"It's okay, girl. I'm not going to hurt your baby." She held her hand forward for the mare to sniff. When the mare planted her soft muzzle in the palm of Ashleigh's hand and blew a warm breath across her frozen fingers, Ashleigh knew the mare was accepting her presence.

The new filly shuffled forward and poked her nose toward Ashleigh, but the move threw her off balance and she fell in a heap again.

Ashleigh stretched a hand tentatively toward the filly, watching for Go Gen's reaction. When the mare showed no objection, Ashleigh ran her hand over the filly's damp coat, starting at her head and working her way back over the body and legs the way she'd seen her parents do.

Go Gen nickered and the new filly scrambled to her

feet, teetering sideways and taking several unbalanced steps to the right before she gained her footing. The foal extended her muzzle toward the mare's flank and made sucking noises with her tongue.

Ashleigh took the opportunity to grab the towel and the iodine. As the filly nursed, swaying unsteadily on her feet, Ashleigh crept forward and coated the stump of the umbilical cord with iodine. Then she began to rub the foal's damp coat with the towel.

The little filly stopped nursing as soon as she felt the towel. She turned to see what Ashleigh was up to, and lost her solid footing. She scrambled to keep upright, her legs flying this way and that before she ran into Ashleigh, using her for a balancing point.

Ashleigh laughed and threw her arms around the foal. "You remind me a lot of Aladdin when he was a baby. He ran over me all the time," she said.

Ashleigh helped the filly back to her dam's side. When the foal was nursing again, Ashleigh sat back down in the corner to watch.

The filly finished nursing and turned to stare at Ashleigh. She shuffled within a few feet of the corner, then plopped down in the straw to take a well-earned rest, while her dam hovered nearby, picking at the flake of hay she hadn't touched during the night.

Ashleigh snuggled deeper into the straw and watched the foal doze. Her eyes grew heavy. Her parents would be home soon. She couldn't wait to show off the perfect new filly. And the next day they'd be flying to Florida to see Aladdin. . . .

Ashleigh's eyes flew open like shutters at the sound of the old truck bumping along the driveway. Had she just closed her eyes, or had she been asleep for a long time? The sounds of melting ice dripping off the barn roof and the warm rays of sunshine streaking in the window told her that she had definitely been asleep.

Ashleigh stretched her sore muscles and grinned when she saw the filly was up and nursing heartily. It was time to introduce her parents to the newest member of the Edgardale family.

Ashleigh heard the barn door rolling on its hinges and crawled from her bed of straw.

"Ashleigh?" Mrs. Griffen's anxious voice echoed down the barn aisle.

"I'm here, Mom and Dad," Ashleigh answered as she let herself out of the stall.

Mrs. Griffen ran to Ashleigh and hugged her, then held her at arm's length and inspected her. "Are you all right?"

"Sure, Mom." Ashleigh shrugged. "Why wouldn't I be?"

Mrs. Griffen squeezed her shoulder. "We called the house as soon as the phone lines were working again. Caroline told us you had spent the night in the barn by yourself. That was a crazy thing to do," she admonished. "We were worried about you."

"I'm okay," Ashleigh assured them, then smiled. "Want to see the new filly?"

Her parents looked at each other, then back at Ashleigh. "You delivered a foal by yourself?" they said in unison.

"Well, Go Gen handled it pretty well. I just watched," Ashleigh said as she opened the door to Go Gen's stall. "Isn't she beautiful?"

Hastily Mr. Griffen rushed into the stall. The filly took one look at his tall form and shuffled quickly to the other side of her dam, peeking out from under Go Gen's tail at the new visitors.

"She's beautiful!" Mrs. Griffen said, laughing at the new foal's antics.

"Looks a lot like Aladdin and Quest," Mr. Griffen observed. "Have you dipped the cord yet?"

Ashleigh nodded. "If Aladdin does well in his next race, and Quest keeps winning, this filly might be a good prospect for Mr. Danworth. Can we take some pictures of her and give them to him while we're down in Florida?"

Mr. Griffen smiled and ruffled Ashleigh's hair. "Let

us worry about the business, Ashleigh. You did a great job delivering this filly. But you really shouldn't have stayed out in the barn all night."

"But what if something had gone wrong?" Ashleigh sputtered. "We can't afford to lose another good foal—not after Midnight."

Mrs. Griffen brushed the hair off Ashleigh's forehead and looked her straight in the eye. "You know how much we love the horses, and how hard it is to lose one," she said. "But what if something had happened to you? You know how easy it is for accidents to happen around the horses."

"Well, I have to admit," Mr. Griffen added, "I probably would have done exactly the same if I were you."

"You are your father's daughter," Mrs. Griffen chuckled.

Ashleigh smiled. How was it that her parents could make her feel loved and in trouble at the same time?

Stardust whinnied, reminding them that it was time for breakfast.

"Ashleigh, your father and I can take care of things in here," Mrs. Griffen said. "The radio said that school has been delayed for an hour. By the look of things, I'm sure you didn't get much math done last night— better use the extra hour to study for that quiz."

Math! Ashleigh had completely forgotten.

8

THE FOLLOWING MORNING ASHLEIGH CLIMBED UP THE steps and into the Danworth's big silver jet with her failed math quiz and math textbook in one hand and her suitcase in the other. This time there would be no chance to read any of the horse magazines the Danworths kept on the jet. Her parents would expect her to study math all the way to Florida, and she could look forward to many tutoring sessions with her favorite person, Peter Danworth, over spring break.

Ashleigh helped Rory into his seat, then buckled herself into her own plush chair. She stared out the window, already missing Stardust and Go Gen's new filly. A whole week without Stardust! And a whole week with Peter. How was she going to do it?

She took out her math book and flipped through the pages, trying to discover where she had gone wrong on the quiz. She thumbed through the explanations, reading them over and over, but they still wouldn't stick in her head. Ask her to name all the Triple Crown winners, or the number one stallion in the nation, and she could tell you without hesitation, but these math problems were just too boring to memorize. She read them again and again, but the night of Go Gen's filly's birth had taken its toll. Soon her eyelids became too heavy to keep open, and she drifted off to sleep.

When the wheels touched down on the runway in Miami, Ashleigh sat up, rubbing the kink in her neck and staring out the jet's small window as they taxied to a stop.

Speaking of pains in the neck . . . In the distance, she could see Peter Danworth standing by the black limousine with a familiar frown placed solidly on his face. He joined his parents as they walked forward to greet the Griffens.

Caroline was the first one off the plane. Peter seemed to brighten and even managed to smile when he saw her, but his frown returned when he spotted Ashleigh.

On the drive to the Danworths' farm, everyone talked at once, making plans for the following week. Mrs. Danworth wanted to drive Caroline, Ashleigh, and Mrs. Griffen into Miami for a day of shopping.

Ashleigh's mother and sister were excited about the prospect, but Ashleigh tried to keep her ears on what the guys were planning. Fishing, swimming, and horses were more to her liking. If she couldn't be at home with Stardust, the Danworths' stable would suit her just fine.

"What about Aladdin?" she asked. "How has he been training this week?"

Peter gave her a dirty look, as if she had no business asking about his horse, but Ashleigh ignored him and turned her attention to Mr. Danworth.

"He was a little tired coming off that last race," Mr. Danworth said. "But he's ready to go again. We've galloped him lightly a couple of times this week. He seems to be doing fine."

Ashleigh looked at Peter. She didn't want to spend a week fighting with him. Maybe she should try to be friendly. "Do you get to gallop Aladdin yourself sometimes?" she asked.

When Peter nodded, Ashleigh breathed a sigh of envy. "You're so lucky. We've got broodmares, and they're really nice, but my parents won't let me ride them. I wish we had a training track and some racers in training like you do."

Peter seemed to warm a little with Ashleigh's wistful comment. He actually relaxed his frown.

She continued, "I've got a mare named Stardust

that's part Thoroughbred. If we had a training track, I could run her around it. She's not as fast as a pure-bred, but it would still be a lot of fun."

"Yeah, it is kind of cool to be able to gallop all the horses," Peter said. "I'm not old enough to get my exercise license at the big track yet, so it's good that I can practice at home."

"What's it like to ride Aladdin?" Ashleigh leaned forward on the edge of the seat.

Peter smiled a genuine smile. "He's really powerful. He's got this awesome stride," he said, sounding enthusiastic for once.

Ashleigh flopped back in her seat. It would be incredible to be able to ride a horse like that. She imagined herself poised over his withers, asking him for more speed.

"We've got some really good horses at our place," Peter said, breaking into her thoughts. "Maybe if I ponied you, your folks would let you ride one of the gentler mares?" he offered.

Now it was Ashleigh's turn to frown. Mr. Danworth must not have told Peter that she was forbidden to ride.

Ashleigh sat forward and spoke in a low voice. She hated to admit it to Peter, but it would be better to tell him herself. "I'm going to be a jockey someday, and I would really love to ride one of your horses," Ashleigh said, noting that the scowl was returning to Peter's face. "But I got in trouble because my math grade was so bad. I can't ride until it goes up."

"That's right." Peter laughed. "Your sister told me you're a real bonehead when it comes to math. That subject is so easy. How could you get a bad grade?"

So much for being friendly, Ashleigh thought. Peter changed moods even more often than Caroline. She'd have to force herself to be nice to him. A plan was forming in her mind, and she needed to be on Peter's good side in order for it to work.

As the limousine pulled into the long tree-lined drive of the Danworths' farm, Ashleigh rolled down the window, letting the warm air and the scent of magnolias float into the air-conditioned car. She breathed deeply, inhaling the scent of green grass and flowers.

Ashleigh was struck by the beauty of the place. Unlike Edgardale's white fences, here the fencing was brown. It crisscrossed over hundreds of acres of green fields, forming large pastures and smaller paddocks for the yearlings and older horses. The Danworths didn't have any broodmares yet, but they had been speaking to her parents about starting a broodmare barn—they certainly had room for it.

The limo rounded a curve and she caught sight of the Danworths' giant two-story brick house, standing like a sentinel between three large barns. The barns were made of gray stone and had black roofs to match the house. Three barns! And she had a whole week to spend in them.

They pulled up at the front door of the house, and Mr. Danworth helped the driver lift their bags out of the trunk.

"You girls have the room at the top of the stairs," Mrs. Danworth said. "Elaine and Derek, we're putting you in the suite down the hall, and Rory can have the room next to Peter's."

"This is so cool," Caroline said as they ascended the long oak staircase. "I feel like Cinderella in a mansion."

Ashleigh smiled. "Yeah, but don't get any dirt on that white carpet, or Mr. Danworth might turn you into a pumpkin!"

The girls giggled as they ran the rest of the way up the stairs to their room.

"Just look at that view!" Caroline said as she threw back the drapes to marvel at the rolling countryside and the huge swimming pool that lay below the south window.

"I like the view from this side better." The window from Ashleigh's side of the room overlooked one of the barns and the training track. Two horses were jogging around the track, but neither one looked like Aladdin.

A soft knock sounded on the door. "Come in," Caroline hollered over her shoulder as she grabbed an armload of dresses from her suitcase and began to hang them up in the spacious closet.

Peter poked his head into the room, running a hand nervously through his sandy hair. "My parents asked me to give you a tour of the grounds. You want to go?" he asked.

Ashleigh had seen that look before. Guys made fools of themselves in front of her sister. She stuffed her clothes in an empty dresser drawer and shoved her suitcase under the canopy bed. "Sure, I'll go. I can't wait to see the barns and all the horses."

Peter continued to look at Caroline as though he hadn't heard a word Ashleigh had just said. He took a step toward her. "Do you want to go, Caroline? I'll show you the swimming pool and the game room, too."

Caroline finally turned her attention away from her clothes and gave Peter a winning smile. "Just a minute. I have one more dress to hang up, and then we can go."

"Can we go to the barns first, though?" Ashleigh asked. "I can't wait to see all your racers." She shucked off her tennis shoes and pulled on her boots.

Peter looked at her as though she had two heads. "Don't you ever think of anything besides horses?

There's plenty of other things to do here. Besides, your sister isn't interested in the horses. Don't be so selfish," he snapped.

Selfish? How could he call *her* selfish? Caroline wanted to look at the pool and not the horses. Wasn't that just as selfish?

"Fine. You and Caro have a great time in the water. I'll find my own way around the barns," Ashleigh replied.

"Suit yourself," Peter said, and held the door open for her to leave.

If Ashleigh could find Mike, the Danworths' trainer, she was sure he'd be happy to show her around the barns and answer all her questions. She sucked in her breath as she walked through the immaculate stable yard toward the training track. Edgardale was wonderful, but this place was spectacular. Someday she would have a farm just like it!

The Danworths had two barns for the racehorses, and another barn for the young horses that had been bought through auction or private sale and were too young to be ridden yet. Ashleigh could see workers already breaking ground to lay the foundation for the new broodmare barn.

She spotted Mike at the rail by the training track holding a stopwatch. She picked a place to stand on the outside rail and waited for him to finish his instructions to one of the exercise riders.

"Hey, kiddo, what's up?" Mike said when he walked over to join her.

Ashleigh smiled up at him. It was nice to see a friendly face after Peter's sour mug. "Is Aladdin working today?" she asked.

Mike kept his eyes on the young colt galloping around the track. "No, it's his turn tomorrow. Mr. Danworth wanted to wait until your family arrived so that your dad could watch him work. This guy here is our last horse of the day." Mike pointed to the chestnut colt, which was straining at the bit, trying to loosen his rider's hold so he could run. "This is his first work. We're going to clock him for a half mile. The rider's just breezing him to see what he'll do."

Ashleigh raised her hand to shield her eyes. She had seen the term *breezing* in magazines and heard it a few times, but she wasn't exactly sure what it was. Mike was the right person to ask. "What is breezing, anyway?" she ventured.

"It's when the rider sits on the horse and lets him run on his own, without the animal's being restrained or asked to go faster," Mike explained. "If a horse is working *handily,* that means the rider has him under wraps and the horse is running against the bit. *Driving* is when a horse is being asked to go all out. The rider will either use the whip or hand-ride him."

"Wow," Ashleigh remarked. "I thought they just ran. Why do they have so many different speeds?"

Mike checked his clock as the rider approached the half-mile pole, clicking the button when the colt's nose came even with the red and white striped finish pole. "Sometimes you just want to put a little air in them without tiring them out too much. And sometimes you want to see everything the horse has got."

Ashleigh watched as the rider rounded the first turn, his body low over the horse's withers to cut the wind resistance. *Someday that's going to be me out there,* she thought. She turned to Mike. "Will Peter be riding Aladdin tomorrow?"

Mike noted the quarter-mile time before answering. "Yes, he rides the colt most of the time at home. He's a pretty good rider, but he seems to have lost interest lately. That's a real shame. I think he'd make a great jockey, but it looks like he's going to outgrow the job, anyway. I guess that's part of why he's been so cranky."

Maybe that's why Peter is so mean to me, Ashleigh thought. *Maybe he's just jealous that I'm small enough to be a jockey.*

The chestnut colt crossed the finish line and the rider stood in the stirrups, leaning back against the reins. Ashleigh smiled. He looked as if he were riding a surfboard, the way he was perched up on the horse's back. You had to have great balance to be able to do that. She'd tried it on Stardust a few times and had almost fallen off.

"Forty-nine seconds," Mike said, and showed her the stopwatch. "That's not bad for a first work. I think this guy is going to be one of our star horses this summer."

Ashleigh felt a wrenching in her gut. Aladdin should be the star horse! "Why isn't Aladdin running better?" Ashleigh blurted out. "I know he can."

Mike leaned on the rail and shook his head. "You've got me there. We've tried everything we can think of. And I must say the colt trains like a champ. He just doesn't seem to put out in the race. He's got that big stride, but he doesn't get anywhere with it. He ends up running clumsily, like a big ol' moose. I was hoping the blinkers would help, but they don't seem to make any difference."

Ashleigh sighed. She had noticed that Aladdin had a funny way of going. He ran with his head up and his legs high. He did look kind of like a moose picking its way through the mud. But she didn't think the colt's running style had anything to do with how badly he was doing in his races. Lots of horses had unusual ways of going. She was still positive the whip was the cause of all the trouble.

Ashleigh looked at Mike, trying to determine

whether he would be upset or laugh at her if she told him what she thought. The genuine smile on his face told her that she could trust him.

"Do you think that maybe Aladdin could be whip-shy?" she asked tentatively. "In the last race it looked like he started slowing down when the jockey really started to stick him."

Mike rubbed his jaw. "That's also about where I expected him to drop out with the fast fractions he set at the quarter poles. He's been sticked in works and it hasn't had any effect on his time, Ashleigh. I don't think that's the problem," he said, shaking his head.

Just then Ashleigh heard footsteps behind them and turned to see who was coming.

"I see you finally found someone to talk horses with you," Peter teased as he and Caroline stepped up to the rail. "Be warned, Mike, that's the *only* topic she likes to talk about."

"What else is there?" Ashleigh said, shrugging. *It's so obvious Peter doesn't really care about horses,* she thought. *He doesn't deserve to own a horse like Aladdin.* It would serve him right if they took the colt back to Edgardale!

"How about math?" Peter reminded her. "Your parents asked me to tutor you. Meet me in the downstairs library a half hour before dinner. We can start then. Come on, Caroline, I'll show you the fish pond."

Caroline flipped her blond hair, glancing at Ashleigh as they turned to leave. "Don't be late, okay?" Peter called back over his shoulder. "We've got a special guest coming to eat with us."

"Special guest?" Ashleigh demanded. She looked at Mike, but the trainer only lifted his shoulders and went to catch the chestnut colt as he pranced off the track.

"I'm not one to spoil a surprise," Mike called over his shoulder, and winked. He began to lead the chestnut colt back to the barn, leaving Ashleigh standing alone at the rail. It was going to be a long week.

9

"GLAD TO SEE YOU COULD MAKE IT," PETER SAID AS HE entered the library and strode purposefully to the chair next to Ashleigh's, picking up her math text and riffling through the pages. "Aw, this stuff is easy. Don't tell me you can't do these problems!"

Ashleigh sat there for a moment, trying to decide what to do. She could feel the burning redness slowly creeping up her face. Did she dare walk out? Peter must have noticed her anger. He handed back her book and tried a different approach.

"I'm sorry," he said in a softer voice. "I just don't understand how someone could have trouble with math. It's so easy."

Ashleigh counted to ten before she opened her mouth—just as her mother had taught her to do. But when she got to ten, she still couldn't think of anything nice to say.

"I'm not stupid," she blurted out. "I get decent grades in everything else. Math is the only subject I have trouble in."

"I didn't say you were stupid." Peter said, his eyes wandering to the library door.

He's probably worried his parents will hear, Ashleigh thought. "Well, you may as well have," she accused. She stood up and began to pace the library floor. "What do I need math for, anyway? I'm going to be a jockey. Jockeys don't need math."

Peter sat forward on the edge of his seat. "There's more to life than horse stuff. Can't you think of anything else?" he demanded.

"What's wrong with liking horses?" Ashleigh countered. Then her temper got the better of her, and she opened her mouth before she could check herself. "I guess it's a good thing you like other things besides horses, since you'll probably be too big to be a jockey."

She flopped back down in the chair and crossed her arms, locking eyes with Peter. At first his glare was cold enough to freeze the swimming pool, but then she could see tears of hurt shining in his eyes. Before the tears began to fall, he scrambled to his feet and fled the room.

"Peter, wait!" Ashleigh called after him. He had treated her with nothing but contempt, but she still felt rotten about making him feel bad. What if *she* found out she was too big to be a jockey? How would *she* feel if somebody rubbed it in her face? Not great—that much was plain.

Ashleigh got to her feet and ran down the hall, trying to catch up with Peter. But he was nowhere to be found. She checked outside the house but didn't have any luck there, either. Then she wandered down to the stables in hopes that he might be hiding out there.

She found him in the first barn, in front of Aladdin's stall. The big black colt had his head over the door, and Peter was stroking his muzzle, speaking softly to him.

"Hey, Big Al, we'll show 'em, huh?" he murmured.

Ashleigh was shocked. Peter had acted as if he didn't even like the horse. But even from where she stood in the barn doorway, she could see that he cared very much. She felt a twinge of jealousy knot her stomach, but she brushed it aside. Aladdin was not her horse. He belonged to Peter. It was only right that he should talk to the colt when he was feeling bad. Just as she talked to Stardust when she was having a bad day.

She ventured quietly up the aisle. "Peter?" she called out.

Peter's head snapped up at the sound of Ashleigh's voice. "Go away," he growled. "Just leave me alone." He turned his attention back to his horse.

Ashleigh shoved her hands in her pockets and

looked away. Apologizing was always difficult, but apologizing to Peter was nearly impossible—he could be such a jerk!

"I'm really sorry," Ashleigh said, looking up at him. "I didn't mean what I said. I hope you do get to be a jockey someday."

She stood there for several moments longer, waiting for his reply. When Peter said nothing, she turned and walked away. There was nothing more she could do. He didn't have to accept her apology if he didn't want to.

Ashleigh returned to the library and picked up her math book. Dinner would be served in a few minutes—there was no more time to study. She trudged up the stairs, still feeling the weight of the rotten things she had said to Peter. Maybe she could skip dinner. She certainly wouldn't feel like eating with Peter's sad face across the table from her.

Caroline was getting dressed when Ashleigh opened the door.

"Hurry up, Ash," Caroline said as she slipped into a bright blue dress. "Dinner's in ten minutes. The special guest will be here any second now." She sat down in front of the dressing table mirror and ran a brush through her blond hair. "He must be someone pretty special, considering all the fuss everyone's making."

"How do you know it's a he?" Ashleigh asked as she

stripped off her clothes and began to put on a clean pair of jeans and a T-shirt.

"Peter said it was a boy our age that he grew up with, so I can't figure out why his parents are so excited. Maybe he spent so much time over here, they feel like he's their son or something." She looked at her watch. "Time to go."

Then Caroline caught sight of Ashleigh in the mirror. "You can't wear that!" she exclaimed, whirling around.

"Why not? This is what I wear at home," Ashleigh said, shrugging.

"The Danworths *dress* for dinner. That means shirts and ties for men, dresses for women," Caroline said in exasperation. "Oh, Ashleigh, what are we going to do with you? You stick out like a sore thumb."

The sound of the doorbell rang through the air.

"There's no time to change," Caroline said as she slipped a pretty gold barrette into her hair. "Tomorrow you can borrow one of my dresses, but tonight you're on your own. I hope Mom and Dad aren't too mad." Then she ran out the door and down the stairs, leaving Ashleigh to fend for herself.

Ashleigh looked in the mirror and frowned. What was all the fuss about? It was just dinner. She rummaged through the dresser and found a button-down blouse. It was the nicest shirt she'd brought. She put it on, careful to tuck it into her jeans, and then bolted down the stairs to the dining room.

The last person had just been seated at the long dining table, laden with sparkling crystal and silver, when Ashleigh screeched to a halt in the doorway. She took a steadying breath and crossed the marble floor, conscious of how ridiculous she looked in jeans when everyone else was so dressed up.

Ashleigh had almost made it to the table when she saw the shocked look on Caroline's face. Then Peter leaned forward to reach for the water pitcher, exposing the Danworths' special guest.

Ashleigh stopped in her tracks. In the chair next to her empty one sat Kevin Donnelly, the handsome star of her favorite television program, *Old Red and Me*. And he was looking right at her. *Kevin Donnelly! Wait until Mona, Lynne, and Jamie hear about this!*

Ashleigh saw the disapproving look on her mother's face when she saw Ashleigh's jeans. She only hoped her parents wouldn't scold her for her outfit in front of Kevin. Then Kevin stood and pulled out the empty chair beside him. Ashleigh relished the look of envy on Caroline's face as the actor pushed the chair in for her when she sat down.

"Thank you," she murmured, blushing.

How am I going to eat with a TV star sitting next to me? Ashleigh wondered. She looked at all the fancy plates and silverware on the table and grimaced. At Edgardale they didn't eat with all these extra pieces.

Ashleigh gazed down at her soup and then looked around the table for a clue as to what utensil to use first. Peter seemed to notice her predicament and grabbed the first utensil to the left of his plate. She smiled her thanks and followed suit, realizing her folly only a moment before she plunged the fork into her cup of soup.

Ashleigh cut her eyes to the side to see if Kevin had noticed. Her heart sank as she saw him politely hide a smile in his napkin. Her gaze shifted to Caroline. Her sister looked as though she wanted to crawl under the table.

Ashleigh placed the fork back on the table and picked up a spoon, but she couldn't bring herself to eat. Her appetite had disappeared. *Peter is such a jerk,* she thought. Then Kevin leaned close and spoke in a whisper that only Ashleigh could hear. "You should see some of the tricks he pulls on me. Don't feel bad. You'll get him back."

Ashleigh smiled gratefully. If Kevin could stand up to Peter's hateful pranks, then she could, too. With that decided, she dug into her soup.

The next fifteen minutes were spent with everyone firing questions at the young actor. Ashleigh was surprised to find out that Kevin lived down the road from the Danworths and went to school with Peter, flying back and forth to Los Angeles to film his TV show.

"So, what are your plans for tomorrow, Kevin?" Mrs. Danworth inquired.

Peter and Kevin traded smiles. Peter spoke up first. "You know Kevin likes to ride whenever he's home."

Kevin nodded vigorously. "I thought maybe we could take the hunters out and show the girls around the ranch."

"Great idea," Mr. Danworth agreed.

Ashleigh's heart sank. She would be left behind. It was so unfair! But how could Kevin know that she'd been grounded? She shot Peter a warning look, took a deep breath, and met her mother's and father's gazes. She'd die of embarrassment if they said anything.

"I'm sorry, I won't be able to go with you," Ashleigh mumbled miserably to Kevin.

"Why not?" Kevin asked, turning to her.

Ashleigh twisted her napkin around and around, trying to think of a way not to embarrass herself. "I promised my parents I'd do a lot of studying while I was here," she replied. "I've got some math to do." She knew the excuse sounded lame, as if she didn't want to ride, which was the opposite of how she felt. She would give anything to go on that ride.

"What about me?" Rory put down his glass of milk

and looked around the table. "I want to ride, too."

"We've got a nice pony that would love to go around the front paddock," Mrs. Danworth said. "He's been waiting for someone his size to come along."

"I can go," Caroline said, flashing a perky smile at Kevin.

Ashleigh stared at her sister. Caroline knew how to ride, but in the last year she had never once volunteered to go riding with Ashleigh. Still, it wasn't every day that Kevin Donnelly rode with them, either.

Ashleigh glanced at her parents. She could see the sympathy in their eyes, but she knew they wouldn't back down on their decision. Hastily Ashleigh finished her meal and asked to be excused.

"Are you feeling all right, Ashleigh?" Mrs. Griffen asked, furrowing her brow.

Ashleigh nodded her head. "Yes. I just want to get to bed early tonight. Mike said they're going to work Aladdin first thing tomorrow," she replied.

"We all want to be there for that," Mr. Griffen agreed. "All right. Good night, Ash."

Ashleigh trudged up the stairs. She knew the rest of the gang was going to play pool after dinner, and she didn't want to hang around listening to them talk about the next day's ride. As she changed into her pajamas Ashleigh tried to console herself with thoughts of Aladdin. After all, that was what they were there for—to find a solution to his poor running performance.

She would just have to spend the rest of her time at the Danworths' sticking close to Mike and Aladdin and trying to figure out why the beautiful black horse wasn't running right. Mike didn't think the whip was the problem, but it seemed as if Mike was looking for a *big* problem to fix, something less obvious than the whip. Ashleigh had read in horse magazines that oftentimes it was the simple problems that caused all the trouble, yet were easily overlooked.

A quick shock of excitement ran through her. The next day she would get to see Aladdin run. Maybe then she would figure it out!

10

ASHLEIGH WAS UP AT THE CRACK OF DAWN. NOBODY else seemed to be awake yet, so she slipped on her boots and silently let herself out of the house. The grooms were just pouring the morning grain when she got there.

"Can I help?" Ashleigh asked the blond young man who was scooping oats into the buckets.

"Sure," he said, and smiled. "We're always happy to have an extra set of hands. Take these buckets down to the last six stalls. Those are the horses that will be taking the day off. They get hay now, too. But the rest of them have to wait until after their workout."

Ashleigh grabbed the buckets and headed down the aisle, smiling as she passed the row of stalls, each complete with a brass nameplate and a halter in the Danworths' stable colors, royal blue and white.

Aladdin poked his head over the stall door and

nickered a greeting. Ashleigh rubbed the white blaze-between his gentle gold-flecked eyes.

"Today you'll run and we'll see if my theory is right," she whispered to the black colt. "Maybe you just don't like the whip, and that's what makes you slow down. Could be that's your problem. Maybe Mike's wrong, huh? Don't worry—I'm going to talk to him again."

She stroked Aladdin's neck and gave him a final pat before moving on to a chestnut mare that looked a lot like Stardust. Ashleigh spent a few extra minutes outside the mare's stall, watching as she munched her grain, and wondering how Stardust was doing back at home. She really missed her mare.

"Good morning, Ashleigh," Mike called as he entered the barn. Ashleigh turned to watch as he led Aladdin out of his stall and put the big black stallion in crossties. He grabbed a light gallop saddle and foam pads from the tack room and began to tack up the colt, placing the saddle pads high on Aladdin's withers and sliding it back a few inches so his coat was smooth beneath.

"How far will Aladdin work today?" Ashleigh asked as she grabbed the white racing bridle and handed it to the trainer.

"I thought we'd go three-quarters of a mile and push him pretty hard. We need to blow a little wind into him. He's got another race coming up this Saturday, remember."

"Will Peter be carrying a whip today?" Ashleigh asked.

Mike smiled. "You're just not giving up on this whip theory, are you?" he chuckled.

Ashleigh looked at the ground, a little embarrassed that she was doubting the trainer.

"I'll tell you what," Mike said. "I'll have Peter go without the stick today, and we'll see what happens. Deal?"

"Deal," Ashleigh agreed, elated that Mike was taking her opinion to heart.

The sound of voices echoed down the aisle, and Ashleigh spun around to find her family and the Danworths walking toward them.

"Are we all ready to go, Mike?" Mr. Danworth called. Behind him, Rory was chattering excitedly. Caroline held his hand, trying to keep him from frightening the horses. Ashleigh's mother and Mrs. Danworth had their heads together, deep in conversation. And Peter trailed the group with the usual sullen expression on his face.

Aladdin raised his head and snorted at the commotion, but Mike laid a calming hand on his neck to quiet the stallion.

"Let's get this over with," Peter said as he put on his

helmet and fastened the chin strap. "Kevin will be here at nine to go riding with Caroline. I need to get our horses ready."

Ashleigh's heart sank. She really wanted to ride with them. "Where are you riding?" she asked.

"Our farm's only a mile and a half from the beach," Peter said as he adjusted the stirrups on the gallop saddle and double-checked his equipment. "A friend of our family owns a big section of private beach. He lets me ride on it whenever I want."

The more Ashleigh heard, the more depressed she got. She would give anything for a ride on the beach!

Peter picked up his stick and pulled on his gloves.

"No stick today, Peter," Mike called, glancing at Ashleigh. Peter shrugged and tossed the stick aside.

Mike undid the crossties and led Aladdin out the barn door. He gave Peter a leg up, and the group followed them down to the training track.

Aladdin entered the track prancing. His jet black coat gleamed in the Florida sunshine as he arched his neck and chomped at the bit. Peter pulled him down to a walk and guided him clockwise around the track. When the colt had settled down, Peter faced him toward the inside rail, making him stand calmly before trotting him off counterclockwise—the correct way around the track.

Ashleigh watched jealously as Peter posted in time to Aladdin's trot and then nudged the black colt into a gentle canter. Peter was so lucky. He had his very own Thoroughbred and his own training track to ride him on—and he didn't even seem to appreciate it! He didn't deserve a horse like Aladdin.

Mike got the stopwatch ready. Ashleigh stood near the rail beside him and her family. The Danworths sat down on the bottom row of bleachers nearby. Ashleigh stood on tiptoe. She wanted to see everything Peter and Aladdin did.

Peter circled Aladdin around the track at an easy gallop and approached the starting pole. The big black colt tossed his elegant head, anxious to go all out. Peter steadied him, then let the reins slacken just a fraction as he settled low over the colt's withers and asked him to run.

Ashleigh's heart pounded and her stomach fluttered as the pair flew by. She felt the drumming of Aladdin's hooves inside her chest as the powerful colt churned up the ground, throwing clods of dirt in his wake. How wonderful it must be to ride such a magnificent horse!

She hated to admit it, but Peter *was* a good rider. He rode just like the best jockeys at the racetrack—nearly motionless, with gentle hands. And he and Aladdin were really flying!

"Come on, Aladdin," Ashleigh shouted. "Show them what you've got!" She watched every move the big colt made, feeling as though she were right there with him. In her mind she could see herself riding Aladdin, stretching him to his limit, the two of them working as a single unit, traveling faster than the wind.

Peter and Aladdin approached the quarter-mile pole by the bleachers. Ashleigh could hear the colt's steam-engine-like huffs as he flew past them, heading for the final turn into the stretch. Ashleigh held her breath in anticipation.

But Aladdin's stride began to go more up and down than forward, his hind legs dragging and his knees flailing. Ashleigh recognized the mooselike way of going that Mike had mentioned. Peter flapped his arm behind him, trying to urge the horse on, but there was no noticeable change. The colt had slowed visibly. Peter gave up and hand-rode to the finish line, scrubbing the reins up and down Aladdin's neck in an effort to drive the colt on.

Mike clicked the stopwatch. "His time's not very impressive. He's going to have to do better than this to get a piece of that race on Saturday."

Ashleigh sighed in despair. Now she wasn't sure she had the answer to Aladdin's problem after all— not if he ran so badly without the whip. She looked at her father, to see if he had noticed anything she'd missed, but he was shaking his head.

"I don't know, Mike," Mr. Griffen said. "One minute he's running like a star, and then all of a sudden he looks like he doesn't know which foot to put down first."

Ashleigh watched as Peter slowed Aladdin to a trot. The horse seemed a little off in his stride as he made the transition, but it was probably just his funny, gangly gait. Despite Aladdin's poor time, he was still breathtaking to behold as he jogged off the track, head held high, mane flying, nostrils flared from the run. He looked like a real pro, despite the sour expression on the face of the boy on his back. Peter was scowling and looked in a hurry to get back to the barn.

As they left the track, a sudden feeling of desperation came over Ashleigh. She just had to figure out a way to get Aladdin to run like a star all the time. It seemed she was the only one who had faith in him now. *If only I could ride him myself*, she thought miserably.

They reached the barn, and Peter unknotted his reins and hopped down from Aladdin, pointing to the white pickup and horse trailer coming down the long driveway. "Here comes Kevin. I'd better hurry."

"Don't be gone too long today," Mr. Danworth said. "We've got some people coming in to look at a couple of our two-year-olds later. I want you to have their stalls cleaned and make sure they're groomed."

"Can't the grooms do it this time?" Peter whined. Ashleigh rolled her eyes.

"Not unless you want to forfeit your allowance this week," Mr. Danworth replied.

Caroline grabbed Ashleigh's arm and pulled her away from the barn. "I'm going to change into my riding clothes. Can you come with me?"

Ashleigh looked wistfully after Aladdin. She wanted to hear if Mike and her father had anything more to say about his performance.

"Please, Ashleigh," Caroline begged. "I haven't ridden in a such long time, and I don't want to look stupid in front of Kevin and Peter. Will you give me some pointers?"

Ashleigh stared at her sister. The desperate look on her face was pathetic—all for the sake of looking good for the boys. Ashleigh had to smile. "Oh, all right. But you owe me for this one," she said.

"Just remember to keep your seat in the middle of the horse and follow her head with your hands," Ashleigh instructed as they walked back to the barn from the house. "You'll do fine, Caro," she assured her sister, looking enviously at the beautiful horses Peter led out

132

of the barn. Ashleigh recognized the little chestnut mare that looked so much like Stardust, and her heart felt heavy—she really missed her mare.

Kevin backed a tall dark bay gelding with a white blaze out of the trailer and began to saddle him.

"He's beautiful," Ashleigh said as she ran a hand over the gelding's glistening coat. "I wish I were going with you."

Peter held the chestnut mare's head and gave Caroline a leg up. Ashleigh could see her sister was blushing as she gathered her reins and adjusted her stirrups. Then Peter mounted his dapple gray gelding. "Well, if you'd spent more time on your math and less time worrying about being a jockey, you could have gone with us, Ashleigh," Peter quipped.

"Why don't you lay off Ashleigh, Pete?" Kevin warned.

"Yeah," Caroline added. "You've been picking on her since we got here. She hasn't done anything to you—leave her alone."

Ashleigh was shocked. Caroline was actually sticking up for her! And Kevin, too. At least she had some allies against Peter.

Peter looked from Kevin to Caroline. "What's the big deal?" he demanded. "She's just a kid." He shifted uneasily when they remained silent. "Oh, all right. I didn't mean anything by it. I'll make it up to her," he said, glancing down at Ashleigh. "If you can think of a favor, Ashleigh, just ask me, okay?" He glanced back at Kevin and Caroline to see if his proposal met with their approval.

"I'll have to think about it," Ashleigh said to Peter. She flashed a grateful smile at her supporters. "Thanks, guys. Have a good ride. I'm going to take Rory fishing—I'll see you later."

Ashleigh thrust her hands into her pockets and walked back toward the house, mulling over Peter's offer. A slow smile spread across her lips. She knew exactly what favor she wanted to ask for, but she'd have to wait for the right time to ask it. She wanted to ride Aladdin!

"You and Rory caught all these?" Mrs. Danworth asked Ashleigh as they sat down to a lunch of fried trout.

Ashleigh glanced at her mother and smiled. "Well, Mom and Dad sneaked down and helped us catch a few." Ashleigh picked at her trout and looked at Mr. Danworth. "Are you going to gallop Aladdin tomorrow?" she asked anxiously.

Mr. Danworth paused with his fork in the air. "We're going to give him a couple of days off," he said. "Aladdin came back this morning with a piece of gravel stuck in his shoe. Mike thinks he's got a mild stone bruise. He figures that may be part of the reason he slowed down at the head of the stretch. But he should be fine in a day or so—it's nothing that will keep him out of that race on Saturday."

Ashleigh grew quiet, considering this information. If Aladdin hurt himself and slowed down at the same time that Peter usually used the whip on him, then she still couldn't be sure if Aladdin was whip-shy or if it was something else entirely. She sighed. There was still hope for her whip theory, but they were running out of time. Now that Aladdin was sore, he'd have to take a few days off. And if she was wrong about the whip, she'd only have four days left to figure out what Aladdin's problem really was. Maybe Mike had some more ideas—she'd have to talk to him once more after lunch.

She found the trainer in the barn where the young horses were. The shed row was perfectly raked, with not a single cleaning tool or monogrammed tack box out of place. The horse barns at the Danworth farm were even neater than Caroline's side of her bedroom at home!

"Back so soon?" Mike grinned as he lead a yearling colt from his stall and hooked him in the crossties. "Peter is supposed to be here to strip these stalls," the trainer continued. "The buyers are due in an hour. Have you seen him?"

Ashleigh swallowed hard. She'd overheard Peter talking to Caroline when they got back from their ride. He'd said he was going to ride his bike over to Kevin's to look at a new horse. He must have forgotten all about the buyers coming in.

Ashleigh bit her lip and wrestled with her conscience. She hadn't forgotten all the mean things Peter had said and done to her. It would serve him right to get in trouble. But she wasn't about to tell on him—she couldn't stoop that low. And besides, he might not be willing to grant her the favor he'd promised if she blew his cover.

"I told Peter I would do his stalls for him," Ashleigh said as she grabbed a blue muck rake off the wall and lifted the handles of a matching blue wheelbarrow.

Mike rubbed his chin, and for a moment Ashleigh was afraid that he could see right through her little white lie.

"I can do them," Ashleigh assured the trainer. "I clean stalls all the time at home. I'm good at it, and I'm fast, too."

"Well, okay," Mike said. "Let me move those colts out to the crossties and you can get started."

Ashleigh worked like wildfire to get the stalls done before anyone noticed. Then she helped Mike groom the yearlings until they glistened.

"So Aladdin got a stone bruise?" Ashleigh asked as they worked.

"Yeah," Mike said, flicking the dust from the curry-comb. "That horse hasn't been much luck. I just hope I'll still get to keep my job here if he doesn't place in the race on Saturday."

Ashleigh swallowed hard. The trainer's face was creased with worry. She liked Mike—she wouldn't want him to lose his job.

Just then Ashleigh heard the squeal of bike tires. Peter wheeled his bike out of the woods and into the entrance of the barn. Leaning the bike against the wall, he walked casually down the aisle, patting the first yearling on the nose. When he caught sight of Ashleigh holding a tail comb, he stopped in his tracks.

Ashleigh was about to explain, but Mr. Danworth rushed down the aisle at the other end of the shed row, nearly knocking Ashleigh over in his haste. Ashleigh watched all the blood drain from Peter's face when he saw his father.

"Those buyers will be here any minute," Mr. Danworth said to his son as he straightened his tie. He glanced at the yearlings. "These horses look like a million bucks. Did you do the stalls, too?" he asked Peter.

Ashleigh let Peter sweat for a second longer before

she spoke up. "Peter did a great job—the stalls all have new bedding," she said, ignoring Peter's shocked stare.

"Great." Mr. Danworth smiled as he placed his hat on his head. "Thanks, son. If I sell one of these colts, you'll get a bonus in your allowance this week. Why don't you and Ashleigh go in and study some math for a while?" he suggested. Then he turned and walked out to greet the prospective buyers.

Peter followed Ashleigh into the library and flopped down in the chair across from her. "You did my stalls?" he asked.

Ashleigh nodded.

"Looks like I owe you big for this one," Peter said. "Why did you do that?"

"I didn't want your dad to miss a sale, and I didn't want you to get in trouble," Ashleigh replied as she peered over the top of her math book to see Peter's reaction. In truth, she would have loved to see him get in trouble, but that wouldn't have helped her get to ride Aladdin.

"I don't believe you," Peter said as he eyeballed her suspiciously. "What are you up to, Ashleigh?"

Ashleigh's heart leaped in her chest. Now was her chance! She sat forward on the edge of her seat. "I know how you can return the favor."

"How?" Peter demanded, raising his eyebrows.

Ashleigh took a deep breath, lifted her chin, and looked Peter right in the eye as she spoke. "I want to ride Aladdin."

11

ASHLEIGH WAITED AS PETER ABSORBED WHAT SHE HAD JUST said, her heart racing at the thought of what she'd just asked for.

Then Peter burst out laughing. "No way!" he cried between peals of laughter.

Ashleigh felt like pelting him with her math book. Did he think she wasn't good enough to ride the colt? "What's so funny?" she demanded.

Peter dried his eyes on his sleeve. "*You* riding Aladdin, that's what's so funny," he chuckled. "You're so little, he'd get away from you in a second." He broke out laughing again.

"I could have told on you if I wanted to—you have a funny way of showing your appreciation, Peter Danworth," Ashleigh said, scowling. "Anyway, I ride just as well as you do!"

Peter got his laughter under control. "Hey, look.

I'm glad that you saved me from getting in trouble," he said. "But I can't let you ride Aladdin. Even if he's not worth much as a racehorse, my parents would kill me. Besides, I thought you were grounded and couldn't ride."

"Who said our parents have to know?" Ashleigh asked.

Peter tilted his head sideways and whistled. "Wow, you must really want to ride him bad."

Ashleigh took heart. Maybe she could wear Peter down if she was persistent. "If I ride him, I think I might be able to figure out what's wrong with him, why he slows down. Please let me try."

"You're just a kid," Peter scoffed. "How would you know anything? My dad and Mike can't even figure out why he's not running."

"But what if I could?" Ashleigh persisted, but Peter only shook his head. "Look," Ashleigh went on, "Aladdin's going to come home with us if he doesn't run well in his next race." The hurt look that leaped into Peter's eyes confirmed her suspicion that he really did love the big black horse, regardless of how he acted. "Wouldn't it be worth a try?" she coaxed.

Peter ignored her question and grabbed the math book from her hands. "That colt is hopeless," he said. "He's never going to run well—there's no point. Come on, we have to do your math."

"Oh, who needs math?" Ashleigh exploded. "I told you, I'm going to be a jockey, and I won't have to use math for that."

"You're right that you'll never use it, because you don't know how," Peter retaliated. "Everyone needs math."

"You're just jealous," Ashleigh huffed. "I can't help it that I'm small enough to be a jockey and you're not."

Peter sat back down and ran his hands through his hair. He heaved a sigh of exasperation. "You're right. I *am* jealous. By the time I'm fifteen, I'll be too big to be a jockey. I've worked hard at it. It's not fair that I'll never get to ride in a real race."

Ashleigh took a deep breath. "I guess I'm jealous of you, too," she admitted. Peter looked up in surprise as she continued. "You've got all these racehorses and your own training track to gallop them on. All we've got is broodmares, one pony, and my riding horse, Stardust. I just wish my family had a place like this."

"Your place doesn't sound so bad," Peter said, and smiled. He extended his hand. "Truce?"

Ashleigh hesitated for a moment. Could she trust him? She would have to if she wanted to ride Aladdin. She shook Peter's hand. "Truce," she said.

Peter smiled. "Now, will you listen to me for a moment?"

"Sure," Ashleigh agreed, and looked at Peter warily.

"Your sister told me that besides wanting to be a jockey, you also want to have your own racing stable someday." When Ashleigh gave him her full attention with an eager nod, Peter continued. "Okay, so say you had twenty horses in training, and each horse got a gallon of oats in the morning, one at noon, and two more at night. How many gallons a day is that per horse?"

"That's four gallons a day," Ashleigh responded instantly. She was confused. *Where is this leading?* she wondered.

"And how many gallons a day would it take to feed all twenty of the horses?" Peter continued.

Ashleigh used multiples of ten and counted on her fingers. "Eighty gallons a day," she answered, although she still didn't understand what he was getting at.

"So if you knew how many pounds of grain was in a gallon, you'd know how much to order for a week's supply of grain, right?" Peter asked.

Ashleigh nodded. She was beginning to see what he was driving at. "But that's not the same thing as—"

"Hold on," Peter interrupted. "What about a jockey's purse? A jockey gets ten percent of the win purse, right? So if the purse was fifty thousand dollars, how much would the jockey get?"

"Five thousand dollars," Ashleigh answered. She

laughed. "But that's not math. That's just horse stuff."

"That *is* math," Peter insisted. "That's why you have to learn how to add, subtract, and multiply. You'll be able to use that stuff for just about everything you do in life, from measuring flour for baking cookies to figuring out what your share of the win purse is when you become a jockey."

Ashleigh felt a flash of comprehension, as if a light had just been turned on in her head. "Wow, I never thought of it like that," she said. "I guess I just had the wrong attitude."

Peter opened up her textbook on the table between them. "See, if we just change the wording of this problem to say 'sweet feed and oats' instead of 'oranges and apples,' and 'Stardust and Aladdin' instead of 'Amy and Billy,' I'm sure you'll get it," he explained patiently.

They went over problem after problem, changing the wording and laughing at the outcome. Over and over Ashleigh found herself producing the correct answer.

When they were almost finished going over all the problems in Ashleigh's old math quiz, Rory pushed through the library door and ran up to Ashleigh with a deck of cards in his hand.

"Can you play a game with me, Ash? Caroline is too busy making goo-goo eyes at that TV boy to play with me."

"I'm in the middle of a math lesson, Rory," Ashleigh said, looking at Peter. She hated to admit it, but she'd actually been having fun doing math.

Rory pouted and turned on his heel.

"Hold on a minute," Peter called. "I think we've done enough math for one day. You guys can play cards on this table if you want."

Ashleigh smiled her thanks at Peter as he got up to leave.

Peter paused in the doorway. "You know, Ashleigh, my dad wants me to take Aladdin to the beach tomorrow," he said. "He wants to take it easy on his foot, but he still need to work, and our track is too hard. Do you want to come and watch?"

"Sure!" Ashleigh jumped at the chance. Somehow she'd have to talk Peter into letting her ride Aladdin.

That night Ashleigh sat in bed with her math book, too excited to go to sleep. She was sure she'd do better on her next math test, and soon she'd be riding Stardust again.

Ashleigh pictured herself riding over the fields on Stardust, then imagined racing down the beach on Aladdin. After a while she felt her eyelids grow heavy, and her head began to bob. She wasn't sure when she had drifted off, but she came awake with a start. The room was dark and Caroline was breathing deeply. Ashleigh lay still, listening to the sounds of the house. She glanced at the alarm clock. It was midnight. She had been asleep for two hours, and now she was wide awake.

Ashleigh lay there for a moment, trying to drift back to sleep, but disjointed thoughts of Aladdin crept into her head. *I hope his foot is better. Racing is dangerous.* She had seen several horses break down during races. Would Aladdin be better off standing at stud at Edgardale, or winning races and letting the world know he was a great racehorse?

She opened her eyes and turned her head to the window. It was a full moon. She thought again of the black colt. There was nothing she'd like better than to have him at home.

Ashleigh felt a prick of conscience. Aladdin had excellent bloodlines, but she knew in her heart that breeders would be leery of a stallion that hadn't proven himself on the racetrack. If the colt could run, he deserved a chance to prove it to the world.

Ashleigh sat up in bed and listened. Except for a few creaks, the house was silent. She swung her feet over the side of the bed and reached for her T-shirt and jeans. Poking her head out the bedroom door, she listened again. It was quiet. She tiptoed down the stairs and out the back door.

The sound of crickets greeted her as she stepped onto the back porch. A full moon was shining brightly, and there was enough light for her to make it to the first barn. Soft grass tickled her bare feet as she padded across the lawn.

It was a warm night, and the barn door was wide open. The moon's rays cast a pale sidewalk of light down the aisle. Several of the horses stirred, giving Ashleigh a curious nicker as she made her way to Aladdin's stall.

"There you are," she called. She opened his stall door and quietly slipped inside.

Aladdin nuzzled her, blowing soft whuffs of breath through her hair. Ashleigh stroked his velvety nose, breathing in the wonderful, warm scent of horse. "What do you think, boy? Would you rather come home with me, or stay here and win races?"

Aladdin lipped her T-shirt and then lowered his head to sift through the straw for a stray piece of hay.

"You're no help," Ashleigh sighed, and ran her hands through his silky black mane, combing out the tangles.

The thin beam of a flashlight streaked across the aisle, followed by quick footfalls on the cement floor. Ashleigh's heart thumped as she ducked below the stall door. The tack room door creaked open, and the intruder rustled around among the saddles and bridles. Were the Danworths being robbed? Ashleigh held her breath, frozen in place. Her heart was beating so loudly, she thought for sure the intruder would hear it.

Aladdin nickered and stepped forward, shoving Ashleigh with his nose. She stifled a gasp as she fell against the door, making a loud bang in the night.

The rustling in the tack room stopped, then the footsteps padded quickly to Aladdin's door. The horse stretched his neck over his door, with Ashleigh crouched below him.

"Hey, Big Al, how are you?"

Ashleigh was shocked to hear Peter's voice. What was he doing in the barn at this hour? She prayed he wouldn't open the door and step inside Aladdin's stall. What would he think if he caught her there?

"Sorry, boy, I'm in a hurry. I'm meeting Kevin for a ride on the beach." Peter chuckled. "And don't tell, okay? I'd be in big trouble if anyone found out."

Peter stroked the white blaze on Aladdin's face. "Someday when you're done racing, I promise to take you—you'd love it," he murmured. His voice took on a sad tone. "That is, if you're still here."

Ashleigh slowly let out her breath as the footfalls receded into the distance. She could hear Peter tacking up a horse at the end of the aisle. Then the door creaked open and hoofbeats echoed down the aisle.

Ashleigh waited until there was no sound for at least five minutes before she moved from her hiding spot. Then she ran down the aisle and across the grass to the house.

She slipped quietly back into her bed, her heart still racing. She was certain she finally had the means to make Peter grant her that favor. This time Peter couldn't refuse her a ride on Aladdin!

The next morning Ashleigh pedaled Peter's mountain bike down the sand path to the beach. When she arrived at the sand dunes, overgrown with tall, waving sea grass, she got off and walked. Riding a horse was definitely easier than riding a bike through sand.

Ashleigh's breath caught in her throat as she topped the dune. The Atlantic Ocean was spread out before her in all its blue glory. Waves crashed on the shore as seagulls strutted up and down the beach, looking for bits of food that might have been washed up by the latest wave. The birds made a racket as Peter circled Aladdin nearby.

"It's about time you got here," Peter called. "I was about to give up on you."

Ashleigh put down the bike and walked toward them, checking that the riding crop hidden in her boot was well out of sight. "He looks ready to run," she said, brushing the hair out of her eyes and smiling up at Peter.

"How come you're so cheerful?" Peter asked.

Ashleigh cleared her throat and shaded her eyes with her hand. "Because today's the day you're going to let me ride Aladdin," she said.

Peter sighed and shook his head. "We've been over this before," he said. "I told you no yesterday. Why would I say yes today? It's a bad idea, and I haven't changed my mind."

Ashleigh kept her gaze fixed on Peter. "Because last night I saw you sneak out to ride one of your parents' hunters on the beach with Kevin." She saw the stubborn look in Peter's eyes suddenly replaced by fear, and knew she had him. "I wonder if your parents would like to know about it," she said thoughtfully, feeling a slight twinge of guilt for blackmailing him. "I could tell them about the stalls I so nicely mucked out for you yesterday, too," she added for good measure.

"You wouldn't," Peter sputtered. He looked worried, and Ashleigh enjoyed the moment.

"Of course I wouldn't," she said finally, and Peter heaved a sigh of relief. "*If* I get to ride Aladdin," she added.

Peter glared down at Ashleigh for several moments before responding. "*If* I let you ride him just this *one time,* you swear you'll never tell a soul about last night?" he demanded. "Or the stalls you mucked out for me?"

Ashleigh crossed her heart with her forefinger. "I swear," she promised.

Aladdin must have felt the tension in the air. He sidestepped down the beach, tossing his head and snorting.

"Whoa," Peter called, and pulled on the reins, frowning as he thought about his predicament.

"I just want to help Aladdin," Ashleigh said, walking toward them as the black horse stepped away. "I know you don't want him to leave, and I don't either, not anymore. If we figure out for sure what's bothering him, he'll start winning races and you can keep him." She held her breath, hoping Peter would let her ride the colt. Even if he didn't, she was sure that she would never carry out her threat to tell on him. It would just be too mean.

Peter kicked his feet out of the irons and leaped from Aladdin's back. He turned to face her, holding the reins out. "All right, Ashleigh," he said. "You win."

Ashleigh's heart soared. "No, Aladdin will win. You'll see!" she cried eagerly, and hurried over to mount up.

The moment Ashleigh touched down on Aladdin's back felt magical. She was so excited, her hands were shaking on the reins. Aladdin felt her tension and pawed at the ground, grinding his teeth on the bit. A small seed of doubt crept into Ashleigh's mind. Would she be able to control him? Aladdin wasn't like Stardust. He felt twice as big and twice as powerful, even at a walk.

"Don't push him," Peter instructed as he adjusted Ashleigh's stirrups. "Just do a slow gallop. If you go any faster than that, he might get away. Trot him off, then break into a canter. He'll pick up the pace on his own. But *keep your reins tight at all times*," he said seriously. "And you need this," he added, handing up his helmet.

Ashleigh buckled the chin strap and turned Aladdin to walk down the beach.

"See that big rock down there?" Peter hollered from behind them. "Turn around when you get to that rock."

Ashleigh trotted Aladdin off, setting her reins low on his neck, just above the withers, and posting in the irons. She couldn't believe she was really riding Aladdin. And it was so much better than any dream she had ever had. She urged the colt into a slow canter, and Aladdin responded perfectly, digging his powerful hooves into the sand.

Seagulls swooped down for a closer look as Ashleigh and Aladdin cantered down the beach, their sharp shrieks joining the sounds of the waves crashing on the shore. Aladdin's black ears moved back and forth, trying to capture all the action he couldn't see beyond his blinkers. The big colt craned his neck, looking for the waves he could hear but couldn't see.

A large wave crashed on the shore, washing close to Aladdin's hooves. Aladdin snorted and lifted his feet high into the air. The next wave covered his fetlocks. Aladdin snorted again, lifting his head and picking up the pace as he galloped across the sand.

Ashleigh remembered the crop she had hidden in her boot, and reached down to pull it out. She didn't intend to use it, but she had to see if Aladdin would quit trying when she showed it to him. She flashed the whip in front of the colt's eyes and gasped at Aladdin's response.

Not only did the black stallion *not* quit trying, but he lunged forward, speeding up several notches and grabbing the bit in his teeth.

"Oh, no," Ashleigh moaned as she felt the colt lengthen his stride even more. Aladdin was running away with her!

12

ASHLEIGH FELT THE WIND RIP THROUGH HER HAIR AS THEY moved faster and faster down the beach. The salt spray stung her eyes, and her heart crept into her throat. If she had intended to work the horse at that speed, she might have enjoyed it, but Aladdin wasn't supposed to be going that fast!

What if he stepped into a hole or stumbled on a piece of driftwood and hurt himself? Ashleigh threw the whip away so she could get a better grip on the reins, but Aladdin didn't slow down.

The scenery flashed by in a blur as they sped by the turnaround rock without slowing down. Grains of sand kicked up by Aladdin's hooves stung her eyes and blurred her vision. The wind whistled past her ears, blocking out the cries of the seagulls that scattered at their approach.

Ashleigh's heart pounded hard in her chest as she

realized it was becoming harder and harder to stay on. He carried his head high, and she recognized the strange, mooselike way of going that she had seen from the ground. Now she knew what it felt like—as if they were climbing an incline. *Maybe he'll slow down,* she hoped.

Ashleigh pulled on the reins again, but her arms and legs were so tired, they felt as though they were ready to fall off. She had never gone this fast on a horse before. What if her rubbery legs gave out and she did fall?

They entered a section of beach that was littered with sticks of driftwood and clumps of seaweed. Aladdin pricked his ears and slowed his pace a fraction, trying to look at all the obstacles in his path. Ashleigh's heart leaped into her throat as Aladdin jumped a piece of driftwood and cut quickly to the left, knocking her off balance. She screamed as she vaulted over the horse's shoulder, grabbing for mane and rein, anything that would keep her from falling. Her hand caught in the brow band of the bridle as she went over, tearing the blinkers from Aladdin's eyes.

Ashleigh hit the ground with a thump and rolled head over heels, collecting sand and seaweed in her clothes and hair. She came to a stop faceup on the beach, her arms and legs spread out as though she were making a Christmas angel in the snow. For a second she couldn't breathe; then a wave crashed over her, filling her mouth and nose with salty water.

Ashleigh didn't have time to think about broken bones as she flailed her arms and legs, choking and sputtering and gasping for air. She got to her hands and knees, crawling out of the waves' reach, spitting sand and salt water as she scrambled to her feet.

When she was standing, Ashleigh looked for Aladdin. She caught sight of him a few hundred yards up the beach, turning around to gallop down the beach toward her.

Ashleigh waved her arms, trying to stop the colt as he approached, but Aladdin dodged her playfully and kept on running, back down the beach toward Peter. As the colt passed, Ashleigh saw that his blinkers had caught on his noseband. Despite her bruised and aching body, Ashleigh couldn't help but marvel at the sight of the black colt, stretched out in a full run, mane and tail flying as he glided over the sand.

Glided? Ashleigh wondered. Aladdin hadn't ever glided when he was at a full run—he usually ran like a gangly moose. But that funny way of going was gone. Ashleigh ran down the beach after him, trying to keep the colt in sight. Aladdin was going better than she'd ever seen him go before, galloping with his head held low, his stride long and smooth. There was nothing mooselike about him now.

Of course! Ashleigh realized in amazement. The blinkers were bunched around his noseband, acting as a shadow roll—just like in the article she had read on the Danworths' jet. The shadow roll was making him lower his head to see over the top of it, and keeping his head low allowed him to travel more smoothly. That was it! That was the key to unlocking Aladdin's potential. He needed a shadow roll!

Ashleigh hobbled down the beach toward Peter.

"Now you've really done it!" Peter yelled angrily when he saw her. He kicked at a shell in the sand and pointed to Aladdin as the black colt disappeared over a dune. "I never should have let you talk me into this!" He turned and ran after his horse, and Ashleigh hurried to catch up.

Aladdin had slowed to a walk, heading in the direction of home, stopping now and then to graze, but always jogging far enough out of range to avoid being caught.

"What're you going to tell your parents?" Ashleigh asked breathlessly as they tried to creep up on the stealthy black horse.

"I'm going to tell them the truth," Peter said. "This is all your fault!" He shoved his hands into his pockets and stared straight ahead at the path, refusing to look at Ashleigh.

Ashleigh's head buzzed as all her thoughts tumbled

one over another, trying to line up in a logical order. "We don't have to tell them that I was riding Aladdin. The same thing could have happened if you were riding him."

Peter halted and spun around. "But it didn't, did it?" he accused. "You just *had* to ride Aladdin. You said you'd figure out what was wrong with him, and now we still don't know," he said dejectedly. "He's going to end up going back to Edgardale. I hope you're happy!" he shouted.

How can he be so mean? Ashleigh wondered. She hadn't fallen off on purpose! She was desperate to tell Peter about her discovery, but he hadn't given her a chance.

"Now he's loose—what if he gets hurt?" Peter demanded, practically in tears as he broke into a run. Ashleigh ran to catch up with him. "Leave me alone!" Peter growled. "I'll catch him myself."

Aladdin had stopped a ways away from them to munch on a patch of succulent sea grass, completely unfazed.

Ashleigh crammed her hands into her pockets, grimacing as her fingers wrapped around a squishy piece of kelp. She followed Peter at a distance, feeling miserable. She had to make this better. She took a deep breath. "I know what Aladdin's secret is," she called to Peter's departing back.

Peter whirled around and stopped, his eyes full of doubt.

"When I fell off, the blinkers got stuck on his noseband," Ashleigh said, walking toward him. "They acted like a shadow roll." She saw the light of hope enter Peter's eyes. "That's why his stride was so fluid and he ran so fast down the beach. That funny gait was totally gone and he was running like a champion—did you see?"

"Yeah, I know," Peter admitted, reaching in his pocket and pulling out a stopwatch. "I clocked him from when he passed you to when he reached me. He *was* moving pretty fast."

"It was the shadow roll, I'm sure of it!" Ashleigh cried.

"You think it might work?" Peter asked, his voice suddenly hopeful.

Ashleigh nodded eagerly. "He's going to win that race on Saturday, and he'll get to stay here with you," she promised.

Peter smiled reluctantly back her and shrugged. "I sure hope you're right about this, Ashleigh," he said. "Look, I won't tell anyone you were riding him now. But if Aladdin really does win, I'll tell everybody that we owe it to you."

Ashleigh hung her head. She wasn't looking forward to facing her parents. She had deliberately defied them by riding Aladdin, and she knew she wouldn't be let off easy. "You don't have to lie for me, Peter. I'll tell my parents the truth."

Peter socked her on the shoulder in a friendly gesture. "Thanks, Ash." He turned and led them through the dunes, following Aladdin's path to the Danworth farm. "Come on, we've got a horse to catch."

Mike and Mr. Griffen were waiting for them when they returned to the Danworths' stables. Peter was leading the colt, the blinkers still bunched up on his noseband, strands of sea grass hanging from the corners of his mouth. Aladdin seemed none the worse for his seaside adventure. Ashleigh walked a little ways behind them, pushing Peter's bike and brushing the sand and dried seaweed from her jeans.

Peter glanced back at her. "Time to face the firing squad," he whispered.

Ashleigh gulped and looked up at her father, trying to judge his mood. He and Mike stood in the aisle, arms crossed, waiting. Ashleigh leaned the bike in the doorway and followed as Peter led the colt down the aisle toward them.

"Looks like you gave him a pretty good workout," Mike commented, his face grim. Mr. Griffen cleared his throat as he studied Ashleigh's face suspiciously. Ashleigh looked at the floor as Peter busied himself with untacking Aladdin. Mike bent down to feel the colt's legs.

"No heat. This guy's got legs like iron," Mike commented, and Peter grunted.

Well, at least Aladdin's okay, Ashleigh thought.

"You haven't been riding him, Ashleigh, have you?" Mr. Griffen asked.

Ashleigh glanced down at her sand-splattered clothes and back up at her father. "Yes," she admitted, her voice barely audible.

"Peter, you let Ashleigh ride Aladdin?" Mike demanded. "No offense, Ashleigh, but Aladdin is a very valuable animal."

Peter looked up from brushing off the colt's legs. "But she figured out what was wrong, Mike," he interjected. Peter reached up and pulled Aladdin's head around for them to see. "See the way these blinkers are all bunched up on his nose? They made a shadow roll," he blurted excitedly. "And when Ashleigh fell off, he ran really fast down the beach. I clocked him—look." He pulled out the stopwatch. "Here's his quarter-mile time!" Peter held out the stopwatch for Mike and Mr. Griffen to look at, but they were both looking at Ashleigh.

"Ashleigh," her father demanded incredulously, "you fell off?"

Ashleigh shrugged. "I'm okay," she answered. "It wasn't his fault."

"Ashleigh Griffen, in case you've forgotten, you have been grounded and are not supposed to be riding!" her father exclaimed, his brow furrowed. "Your mother and I cannot tolerate your disobeying us like this. If you ever want to ride Stardust again, you are going to have to shape up and start acting responsibly!"

Ashleigh looked at Peter helplessly. It didn't sound as though her father was interested in how fast Aladdin had run on the beach.

"But she figured it all out!" Peter interrupted. "Aladdin's going to win his race on Saturday. With the shadow roll," he insisted. "If it weren't for Ashleigh, he wouldn't have had a chance."

"Whether he'll win or not remains to be seen, Peter. Come on, Ashleigh," Mr. Griffen said. He grasped her elbow and began to lead her down the aisle, shaking his head. "You could have been killed out there. Your mother is not going to like this one bit."

Ashleigh followed her father reluctantly. Behind her, she heard Peter say, "Give him a chance, Mike. Please."

And Mike's reply: "It may be our only hope."

When Saturday morning arrived, the Danworth house was full of excitement. This was the day Aladdin would prove himself! Everyone piled into the limo and talked nonstop all the way to the backside of the racetrack. Even Kevin had come to watch the big race.

When they arrived, the grooms had Aladdin in the crossties and were working on his coat. Ashleigh and Caroline hurried over to braid blue carnations into his mane and tail.

"Just a couple more in his forelock," Mrs. Griffen said as she handed two more flowers to Ashleigh.

"He looks like a sissy," Peter complained, and Rory agreed with him.

"Maybe they'll make him run faster," Caroline said with a giggle.

"You want him to look good for the win photo, don't you, Peter?" Mr. Danworth said, handing Mike the white racing bridle with the new shadow roll attached to it. But from the worried look on his face, Ashleigh could tell he wasn't at all confident of the outcome of the race.

"That's the spirit," Kevin said cheerfully as he nudged Peter with his elbow. Peter looked worried.

"The times this guy's been clocking with the shadow roll have been pretty good," Mike said. "I think we've got just as good a chance of winding up in the winner's circle as any other horse here today."

He'll win, Ashleigh thought. *He's got to.*

"There's the call to the gate," Mr. Danworth said nervously. "It's time to go."

They followed Aladdin and the pony horse to the front side. Ashleigh couldn't take her eyes off the black colt as he circled in the saddling ring. He was by far the best-looking horse there.

The paddock judge called for the riders to mount up, and Ashleigh felt another boost of confidence. The Danworths had hired Rhoda Kat to ride Aladdin. She had been the winningest jockey at the Gulfstream meet and had just moved into first place at Hialeah this season.

Ashleigh watched the way the jockey handled Aladdin, steadying the reins and talking softly to the colt. Ashleigh couldn't keep the grin off her face. *Someday that's going to be me!*

"Let's head on up," Mr. Griffen said as he ushered them toward their seats. He gave Rory a wink that said he knew he'd rather be outside, but they had to stay with the Danworths. Once again Mr. Danworth had insisted they watch the race from the Turf Club. Ashleigh trudged up the steps, wishing she could be down on the rail screaming with the rest of the racing fans as the horses flew past.

Ashleigh sat between Caroline and Peter in the cushy booth. Kevin sat beside Caroline, with Rory next to him. The Danworths, Mike, and Ashleigh's parents sat in the next booth.

"Doesn't Aladdin look amazing?" Ashleigh breathed

as the black horse trotted off in the post parade. Aladdin pranced and put on a show for the crowd. His odds were still high, but he looked every inch a winner.

Ashleigh glanced at Peter. He gave her a shaky smile and a silent thumbs-up, clearly too nervous to talk. They were friends now, and Ashleigh was glad of it. When Aladdin won this race, there would be a lot more races for him to run after it, and she was planning to see Aladdin and Peter in the winner's circle every chance she could get!

She focused her attention back on the track. They were loading the horses into the starting gate. Ashleigh held her breath as Aladdin balked, refusing to go into the gate. Then two men from the crew got after him and he walked in without any more fuss. Soon all the horses were loaded.

"They're all set," the announcer called. "And they're off!"

There was a collective gasp at the table as Aladdin broke poorly from the gate, settling in dead last as they ran down the stretch and into the first turn.

"Oh, no," Peter groaned, his head in his hands. "He's in last place again. There's no way he can make up all that ground."

"It's just the beginning, Pete. There's still time," Kevin reassured his friend.

"It's okay," Ashleigh said confidently as she watched the colt even out his stride. "Both his sire and grand-sire liked to come from behind."

"But look, he's running smoothly," Mike pointed out. "See how easily he's going? Maybe the shadow roll will do the trick after all."

Aladdin was still in last place as they raced around the far side of the track. Ashleigh was beginning to worry. She stood up in the aisle to get a better view, and Peter joined her. "Come on, Aladdin," she whispered, but the big colt stayed where he was, trailing the pack.

Peter flopped back down in his chair and looked away from the race. "It's happening all over again," he said, staring down at the table.

Kevin stood up and clapped Peter on the back. "Come on, bud. It's not over yet. Get to your feet," he shouted. "Aladdin needs all the help he can get."

Ashleigh exchanged a worried look with Caroline, then locked her eyes on Aladdin as he headed into the final turn. "Please, Aladdin," she pleaded. "You can do it. You've got to win this race."

As if the black colt had heard her plea, Aladdin began to creep up on the horse in front of him, stretching out his stride and gaining more ground in the final turn. He passed that horse and began to move up on the next one. The jockey waved her whip in the air, and Aladdin surged forward, passing yet another horse.

"Royal Jester is in the lead, with Magic Purpose running second," the announcer cried. "And now it's Aladdin's Treasure, making a move from the back of the pack!"

"Go, Big Al!" Peter screamed beside her, and Ashleigh slapped him a high five.

Kevin, Caroline, and Rory moved into the aisle to join them, jumping up and down when Aladdin passed yet another horse.

"Royal Jester is still in the lead, but Aladdin is moving up on the outside and coming on strong," the announcer called.

Aladdin took the turn wide, passing the second- and third-place horses on the outside. He caught Royal Jester and passed him with a sixteenth of a mile still to go. But he didn't stop there. Opening up, he increased his lead by nearly four lengths, galloping through the finish in record time!

"It's the outsider, Aladdin's Treasure, by three and seven-eighths, with the odds-on favorite, Royal Jester, running second and Time to Go running third," the announcer called.

"He won!" Peter shouted, hugging Ashleigh.

"We did it!" Ashleigh cried, hugging him back.

"Come on, everybody! Follow me!" Mike called, leading the way to the winner's circle.

Ashleigh rushed to follow him, feeling giddy with happiness as everyone pounded down the steps.

Rhoda Kat beamed from Aladdin's back in the winner's circle, and Peter held the black colt's reins, smiling proudly for the cameras. Aladdin pawed the ground and shook his elegant head as the photographers' cameras flashed.

Ashleigh's heart swelled with pride to see Aladdin in the winner's circle. She couldn't wait to tell Go Gen's filly all about her wonderful older brother.

"He did it!" Peter crowed. He passed the reins to Mike and nearly strangled Ashleigh in another grateful hug. "You did it!"

"Congratulations!" Mr. Griffen said, shaking Mr. Danworth's hand and clapping Mike on the back. "Guess we won't be needing that stallion contract now," he joked.

"No," Mr. Danworth said, "but Peter and I want Ashleigh to have a free breeding to Aladdin for the mare of her choice. After all, the shadow roll was her suggestion."

Ashleigh was so thrilled she couldn't speak. Her mother beamed proudly by her side.

"I think we'd better take a look at Go Gen's new

filly, too," Mrs. Danworth said. "The one you showed us pictures of. I'm sure Aladdin wouldn't mind having a sister in the barn, once she's old enough."

"Shadow," Ashleigh heard Rory say behind her. She turned to see Rory looking up at Aladdin with his blond head cocked.

"What was that, Rory?" she asked her brother, laughing. Amid all the excitement, Rory looked calm and thoughtful.

"That's what I'm going to call Go Gen's filly," Rory said. "Shadow."

"That's perfect, Rory," Mrs. Griffen said.

"And don't forget," Kevin called over. "Rory said he has first choice for the TV for an hour every night for a week. He promised he'd pick *Old Red and Me*. At least I know I've got one fan." Everyone laughed, but Ashleigh knew from the look on Caroline's face that Kevin had more than one fan.

"Come on, everyone. Group picture," Mr. Danworth called.

Ashleigh went to stand near Aladdin's head and laughed when the black horse nuzzled her hair. From the pleased smiles on her parents' faces, she knew she'd been forgiven for riding Aladdin. And now that math was making more sense than ever, she was sure to be riding Stardust soon enough. She thought about the promise Mr. Danworth had just made: a foal out of Aladdin. She knew just which mare she would want to breed him to. The thought of Stardust running in the pasture with a black foal at her side brought a big smile to her face, a smile that would remain forever in the press photos of Aladdin's first win.

CHRIS PLATT rode her first pony when she was two years old and hasn't been without a horse since. Chris spent five years at racetracks throughout Oregon, working as an exercise rider, jockey, and assistant trainer. She currently lives in Reno, Nevada, with her husband, Brad, five horses, three cats, a llama, a pot-bellied pig, and a parrot. Between books, Chris rides endurance horses for a living, and drives draft horses for fun in her spare time.